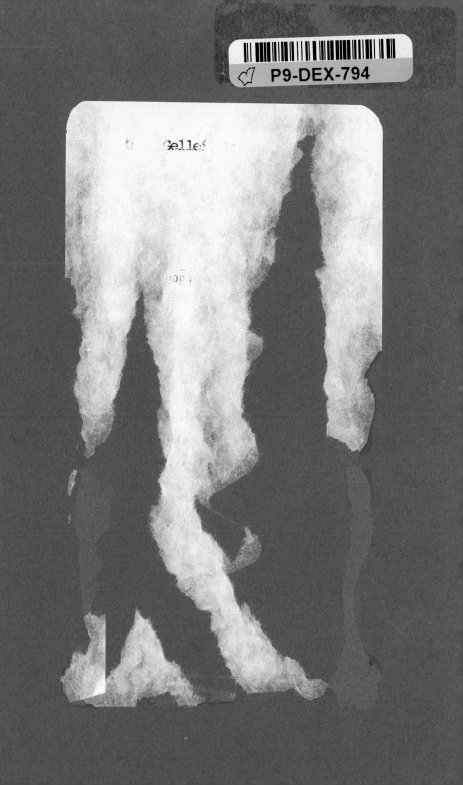

GAD

Previous novels by Stephen Geller

She Let Him Continue
Pit Bull
Joop's Dance

GAD

a novel by

Stephen Geller

HARPER & ROW, PUBLISHERS

New York, Hagerstown, San Francisco, London

FIRST EDITION

Designed by C. Linda Dingler

Library of Congress Cataloging in Publication Data

Geller, Stephen.
  Gad, a novel.
  I. Title.
PZ4.G3216Gad 1979   [PS3557.E4]   813'.5'4   78–69620
ISBN 0–06–011493–2

---

79 80 81 82 83 10 9 8 7 6 5 4 3 2 1

To My Teachers, the Women in My Life:
Polly Hillary and Joan
and
Prayerchord and Her Sisters

ATEH MALKUTH VE'GEBURAH VE'GEDULAH, LE-OLAM. . . . AMEN

Acknowledgments

The author is grateful to Rosemary Torigian for her patient service and helpful comments; to Harvey Ginsberg for his editorial advice; to Phyllis Seidel for her encouragement and support; to le famiglie Grimaldi-Gubinelli of the Antico Caffé Greco e con i suoi camerieri Sigri. Ezio, Domenico, Giulio e Carmine; to Margot and Malcolm McDowell for their friendship; to Jake and Sharron Jacobsen, Rusty McCann, Nancy Nicholas, Melanie Toyofuku, Phyllis Shlemmer, Israel Carmel, Sir John Whitmore for their help on all planes; to Tezrael, who knows where I am; finally, to Oshan, Arigo, Astranine and Huva, servers of The Nine.

WAHE GURU!

PART
ONE

Now I shall tell of things that change, new being
Out of old.

—Ovid, *Metamorphoses*, Invocation

1

Oliver Gad is dreaming:
Dorset, the lapping dapply fields beneath quick-paced, lowering clouds. The chalky Giant of Cerne Abbas, phallus erect, club aloft and about to swing at the storm-filled sky gathering off Weymouth esplanade. Is there time to descend, on his dreamflight? A cream tea's awaiting by Dorchester High Street?

A knock at the door, bold and booming. The phallus descends; the club turns gray; cream tea dissolves in the ether.

"Ollie?" calls Gwyneth, amused by his loin stir beneath the sheets. She tosses back a lock of her coppery hair, and he the quilt.

"It's the door. . . ." Gwyneth Powys smiles, rearranging the quilt, refusing to note the annoyance in his eyes. He smooths the coppery hair upon her shoulders, consciousness at fingertips. She is as soft as summer grass, her eyes sea-green emeralds.

"Wait for it," she whispers, and licks his middle finger.

Oliver Gad takes the dressing gown—yes, as gray as his hair; how so, at thirty-six? "The Silver Fox of Lombardy Street" the *Times* had called him—and crosses to the door.

"Who knows we're at the Brace of Pheasants?" he whispers worriedly.

3

Gwyneth shakes her head. "I told no one we'd be in Plush. . . ."

Again the knock, distinct and slightly unsettling.

"Bloody damn," mutters Oliver Gad, and opens the door.

There are two of them: a short man with a wizened face and a giant, shuffling beside the small man.

"Mr. Gad?"

But Oliver shakes his head.

"The name's Wilson."

The short man is surprised.

"I'm sorry, sir. We know it's Gad."

Oliver starts to close the door as the lights explode and a murderous clock tower booms behind his left ear.

Strange, but he seems to hover above himself, to watch himself being lifted onto the giant's shoulder like a sack of coal, then hauled to a waiting car, a Rover color of burgundy. Then the situation seems banal from his shifting vantage point; he turns away from his physical self and begins to float toward a path at the end of which is an altar. Beside the altar stands a woman, in the crescent of the moon.

Lights flicker above his face. Someone is putting ice to his head. Sticky. Tickling and oppressive. He feels like a beached and bloated whale. Oh, to be a Florentine angel! Oh, to be the soul of St. John!

"Good morning, Mr. Gad."

Partly from petulance, partly from a heady sense of his own survival, Oliver says nothing. He tries to focus upon the speaker, deliberately allowing himself time to recover, to play for time, to bargain in silence. The other men have disappeared. Gad is in a gray room with the sound of traffic close at hand. Is there a window?

The man beams a smile—the light, does it come from his smile?—and Oliver can sense a wave of cold intelligence creating a chilly field about him. Oliver puts a hand to his ear.

4

"When they hit you, Mr. Gad, what did you see? A v
beside an altar?"

Oliver focuses. Shocked.

The man is of medium height, with doe eyes. Soft and l
Liquid and intelligent. His hair is full, rich. Beard full a
His nose is as imposing as the Salisbury spire. His rhyt
speech is public school, but his manner street-electric. He
tan pants, a Norfolk jacket, checked shirt and tie. A Lor
doing the country weekends. Bollocks, Gad decides. A di

"I am called Sefer, Mr. Gad. It means Book, if you rem
your Hebrew."

Oliver smirks. Says nothing.

"Our Gwyneth is fine," the man continues. "You're a
up at the Brace of Pheasants, and Mrs. Powys is on he
to Wales."

Wales?

But Oliver nods, ever so politely, ever so correctly.

"Needn't worry about her husband, Mr. Gad. Or h
already told you of the divorce?"

Oliver thinks: One physical body blow, three emotiona
and what do *I* have to counter the attack? Silence? Dar
silence!

"Well then," Sefer continues pleasantly. "Will we n
bargain, Mr. Gad?"

Oliver sighs. "What do you think I've the need to k
for?"

Sefer hands Gad a packet of Silk Cuts #3. His own j
Had Gwyneth stuffed them into his pocket as he lay
across the giant's shoulders? What a witch! And hummir
loveliest witch of the West Count-ree. . . .

"Mr. Gad? Please pay attention. One year ago, in Pa
Underground driver crashed into the end of the line,
himself and thirty-seven passengers. At first the autl
thought he'd had a heart attack, but an autopsy prov
theory false. Several psychologists suggested suicide, ye

interviewing his family and his parents, they had to discredit that conclusion. A group of engineers studied the automatic cutoff of the train. It's set electrically, you see, and sealed for just such an occurrence. It had neither shorted nor been tampered with. To many, the accident still remains a mystery."

Gad shuffles in his chair. He brings the matches out of his pocket and reaches for the cigarettes. He toys with the packet.

"Six months ago," Sefer continues, "the satellite tracking dish at Malta melted for no apparent reason. Specialists were brought in, analyses made, and a most curious report sent back to Brussels: the molecular structure of the dish had been altered to a degree impossible to accomplish by technological means."

Gad flicks a cigarette from the packet, pops it into his mouth. His hands are shaking for no conceivable reason.

"Finally, as you may have read, the Chinese have told the West how to predict earthquakes, how to deal with vast population movements before such quakes occur. And yet, three months ago, a quake of vast proportions caught the Chinese totally off-guard. All the seismologists were absent from Peking when the devastation occurred. Strange, don't you think?"

Gad lights the cigarette, inhaling deeply.

"Paris, Mr. Gad, Malta and Peking. What do these three cities have in common?"

Gad stares at the ceiling reflectively, then blows the smoke toward Sefer. "Small dogs, I would imagine."

Sefer removes a pistol from his shoulder holster. He sets it between them.

"Stare at that gun, Mr. Gad. Connect your eyes to it."

Oliver snorts, but he stares at the pistol on the table.

Weirdly, it begins to shift, to turn one-quarter of an inch in his direction without either man touching it. Oliver laughs, gazing wide-eyed at the pistol. But the other man is frowning.

"That's what I thought," says Sefer grimly. "You're a time bomb. And you don't even know it."

Pity Ollie Gad, the pretty one, the walking example of Warhol's declaration that everyone in the world will be famous

6

for five minutes. He'd thought of his odd abilities as a gift and would have thanked the Bestower had he known of or believed in His address. Becoming used to his own gift, however, at times even yawningly bored with it, he had begun to rationalize the ability as something genetic; that explanation soon retreated to allow other explanations, more expeditious, to supersede the first. His knack was replaced by "insight," his insight replaced by "intellectual integrity," his integrity tempered by "knowing the right people and playing the game" until the gift as a precious extension of his otherwise normal sensory range had been buried to allow Oliver Gad to appear as insular as Albion, and as superficially polite.

It had taken a witch to sense the treasure, perhaps to begin the careful digging. Would Sefer's drill be equal to the task?

"Who are you?" whispers Oliver Gad.

"I work in a minor branch of Intelligence. A psychic branch. It's a bit peculiar, Mr. Gad, for it presumes that mind *energy* will replace mind product as the next weapon. Those three examples I cited are proof of the validity of our thesis."

"*Right*," Gad snarls. "And I presume you've learned a great deal about me from Mrs. Powys. You've taken the trouble to trace my movements. Dragged me unconscious from an inn. . . ."

"The woman of the moon," Sefer smiles.

"Yes," snaps Oliver. "And you've read my mind. I dream of women." He smirks, furious now, ragingly angry with Gwyneth. "Moon's creatures. Born of one, taught by another, betrayed by a third, succored by a fourth, and at this rate I'll probably die at the hands of a fifth."

"You needn't be so testy, Mr. Gad. I merely read your dream."

"What is it you want?"

"The answer to a question."

Oliver raises his eyebrows. "One?"

"Only one."

"And will it lead to others?"

Sefer smiles slightly, shaking his head. "Bear in mind, Mr. Gad, I'll know you're lying. And if you lie, I might even ask Gwyneth's permission to shoot you."

Damn the woman, damn Mrs. Powys! He'd met her at Boulter's; he'd chatted her up in front of her stuffy husband. When he asked her what she did, when she replied she was a witch, he'd wanted her on the spot, he needed her, though he didn't know why. Oh, and twice she'd let him take her, and wasn't this supposed to be the best of all possible weekends, with longer weekends to come?

She had been the first woman he'd been with in a year who hadn't requested his birth sign. Most likely because she already knew.

They order tea, more ice for Gad's ear. Sefer knows exactly how he likes tea. With scones and clotted cream. Tart gooseberry jam. Mouth stuffed, Oliver watches. Mouth empty, Sefer begins.

"You were an accountant for Midvale Industries. From 1962 to 1968. Rose quickly to seniority position. Met Sir Bill Boulter, suggested purchasing six thousand shares of Glasgow Petrol three months before the North Sea discovery. Six months later you suggested he drop it."

Gad smiles coldly, unimpressed. "And before that?"

"Born in Liverpool, 1941. Working class. In 1958, London School of Economics. You know the route. Boulter delighted with your advice. Forms a Consortium of investors in 1968 with Mr. Gad, the Silver Fox, as private adviser. In 1969, you leave Midvale. Thousands of young men pass through the portals of LSE, Mr. Gad, filled with knowledge of growth-rate methods, forecasting techniques, investment cycles, the lot. Some have no sense of timing whatsoever; others are thirty or forty percenters. Boulter was correct to hire you. In the course of nine years, Mr. Gad, you have earned the Consortium nearly sixty-three million pounds. You hit over *ninety percent.*"

"What do I receive for my service?"

"Two percent of the first five million. Three and a half, from five to ten, and so on. At present you have arrived at twelve and a half percent."

Oliver pales. "I pay taxes."

The man smiles. "You're a Socialist, Mr. Gad. Nobody denies it. Yet your predictions are responsible for putting over three hundred thousand workers in the engineering industry out of jobs. You've also forced the resignations of six company chairmen, three MPs, and can legitimately be pointed to as the one man responsible for half a dozen suicides."

Old history, thinks Gad, and shrugs for Sefer's benefit.

"I'm sure you can make a leftist case for the resignations; certainly I can make a strong case for the necessity of the suicides. Nobody misses *those* bastards, Mr. Gad, not even their families. As far as putting the three hundred thousand people out of work, there isn't an ecological group in the kingdom that doesn't secretly thank you, though the Unions would see you dead. So you have it both ways. Were Shaw alive, he would have written you as a lovable bastard, lacking in nothing but Christian charity—which would have been the final irony, of course, since you've given away sixty percent of your declared money to the government and to various foundations and arts councils. Being optimistic, I prefer to think of those gifts as guilt."

Oliver sets the scone upon the tray and daintily flicks a piece from the corner of his mouth.

"Guilt?"

"Of course. For those undeclared accounts of yours in Curaçao, Guatemala and Liechtenstein. I don't blame you, of course. Had I the wherewithal, I'd probably do the same."

Gad says nothing. How in hell had Sefer learned? Not even Boulter knew!

"Not to mention the Singapore—"

"All right, Sefer, and you may not believe it, but the reason I've made so much money is that I've no respect for it."

"I believe you. Your private self—what Mrs. Powys would call your Higher Self—is concerned with other matters. However, you do have a public face, and that's the one to be tweaked if need be."

Blackmail, then, thinks Gad. But of course.

"May we get on with the question?" he asks.

"Certainly. *Why do you do things in threes?*"

He'd never thought about that. There was never thinking. Just doing. Tingling electrically. Knowing and then later wondering why, and then even later creating the *post facto* rationale.

As he read the index, scanned the names of companies, his right hand tingled or did nothing at all. Right hand picked up the order; brain channeled it; orders flowed. And it was done in threes, yes. Three thousand shares, nine hundred shares. He'd been at Midvale *six* years, before he'd left. Nine years now with the Consortium. And here he was, having a conversation at 9:00 A.M., thirty-six years old, and his right hand was trembling from the question *Why do you do things in threes?*

Oliver thinks: He knows my past. He reads my dreams. Why does he ask a question I can't answer? And who is the woman by the altar? I remember traveling in sleep: Dorset, the Abbas Giant. Even the Dorchester tearoom. Then being knocked on the ear and actually watching myself being carried to the car. Turning to a dark and silvery path. An altar in the distance, with a woman. Two of me: the physical and the *what?* What do they call it? *If* I saw myself being knocked unconscious, then the woman on the path is as real as the Rover color of burgundy.

"They brought me here in a Rover," he says.

Sefer nods.

"A dark color. Burgundy, wasn't it?"

Again, Sefer nods. "The answer, Mr. Gad. Why is everything you do in threes?"

Oliver sighs. "Honestly. *I don't know.*"

For a moment the man called Sefer does nothing. Then he picks up a copy of *Investors Chronicle,* opens to a page and says, "Tell me what will jump six points next week."

Oliver grins, putting the journal on the table. Holding his hand over it, scanning. Nothing. He feels nothing. Then a tingle.

"A movement in gilts: Exchequer thirteen pc1980. No great investment, though. Short fund, with two and a half years' interest. You could make six point nine. . . ." He stops himself. He is trembling, tasting sweat at his lip. "Jesus God. . . ."

"Be careful, Mr. Gad. Your ignorance has cosmic implications."

Oliver looks up worriedly. Sefer smiles, for Gad resembles a schoolboy caught in onanistic play. Yet it is as if the schoolteacher had suggested a trip to a brothel instead of a caning, all expenses paid.

"Sefer, *what does this mean?*"

"Turn to the next page, please. Run your hand over commodities."

Gad does so, thinking: He's seen my hand anyway. He's seen everything, the bastard.

"And what do you find?"

Oliver takes a breath.

"Diamonds . . . anything producing crystals . . . the next twelve years will see a rush on tins, metals. Short-term investments. The real gains are in crystals. . . ."

He closes his eyes: seeing the crystal within. Coming up short. Breathing hard. Sefer nods, slowly, letting the young man bathe in his own confusion.

Oliver Gad is staring at him, wide-eyed, knowing unconsciously that he must play the Apprentice to Sefer's Sorcerer.

"What do you want from me? Certainly not tips. . . ."

But Sefer does not move, remaining eye-locked, now, in the moment.

"Mr. Gad, have you ever looked back upon your investments, seen a pattern to them?"

"About doing everything in threes?"

"No. About what you've bought and sold."

"Other than the immediate stream of events," Gad spits, drawling like a squire, "the sociopolitical bit, the implications

11

of our joining the European Economic Community? Want a
bit of psychoeconomic history, Herr Doctor?"

Sefer refuses his irony.

"I'm talking about a pattern, Mr. Gad. If I could look back
upon my life, upon my behavior, certain patterns would
emerge. You've a very tangible history in terms of what you've
bought and sold. I can take the nine years of the Consortium
and make sense of them. So can you, if you try."

"The psychoanalytic economist, that's your game, is it?"

"If it were so, Mr. Gad, we'd have nothing to discuss."

"What is it then?"

Sefer opens a briefcase—funny how Oliver hadn't noticed—
and pulls out the Consortium's portfolio of investments, to toss
it to Gad.

"I'll give you half an hour."

Sefer rises, leaves the room, locking the door behind him.

In a half hour's time, Gad can find no trace of any kind of
pattern. Nothing but his own successful chaos in the mar-
ketplace.

"Then let me tell you," Sefer begins. "The general pattern
is quite simple: to do away with the twentieth century. To
bring in the twenty-first."

"How so?"

"By encouraging those areas which sustain rather than de-
plete life-support systems; by forcing development in solar as
opposed to nuclear research; by forcing the acquisition of prop-
erty less for commercial and industrial than for agricultural
development. Shall I go on?"

"Bollocks. *Half* of last year's activities were in chemicals,
in engineering firms."

Sefer smiles, appreciatively.

"Bought low, dumped high, and the companies sent spinning
into crises. With, let me add, a goodly portion of the gain rein-
vested in new companies with long-term growth. Companies
with a peace mentality, Mr. Gad. Take Bright Aluminum."

Gad doesn't remember Bright at all.

12

"In 1971, a statement of public offering in the *Financial Times*. You purchased six hundred thousand shares at forty-five pence each. They're now worth two hundred and fifty-two pence."

"In six years?" Gad snorts. "Sell them."

"But do you know what Bright makes?"

"Aluminum, obviously."

"Solar condensers, Oliver, don't be so naïve. Admittedly, eighty-five percent of its weight is in the usual staying-alive, staying-put nonsense, but fifteen percent *is* in research. Note that."

"Noted. And fifteen is also divisible by three."

"Correct. And one plus five is six. Fifteen percent in research, led by Dr. Grant Beardsley, Nobel Prize in Physics, one of Cambridge's bright young men. Did you know that he was to be hired in 1972, less than a year after the Bright's offering?"

"No."

"Do you wish me to continue? Because there is a connection, Oliver."

Gad stretches, more from nervous exhaustion than from physical fatigue.

"I'm not the least bit mystical, you know."

"I'm not so sure. . . ."

"Figured you weren't," snorts Oliver. "All right, then: I'm actually a saint in disguise, sent by God to lead Britain into the twenty-first century, though I cause havoc in the twentieth. Stop me, Officer, before I burn the Church of England."

Sefer rises.

"You may be closer to the truth than either of us would care to imagine."

"For a man with one question, you've asked a dozen."

"It's my work. I'm quite good at it."

"What do you want from me, Sefer?"

"For a time, I'd like you to be one of ours."

"What makes you think I want to be one of *anybody's?*"

Sefer smiles, with a hint of sadness. "The same thing that made you give me an honest response to my question: a strong

13

sense of survival. Well then. Will you agree to a holiday in Wales? Or must we set eyebrows raising at the Inland Revenue?"

Oliver rises, beginning to pace.

"What's in Wales?"

"More questions. And, for your recreation, the wooing of a witch named Gwyneth."

On the rain-wet road to a village in Wales:

"Why am I a time bomb?" asks Oliver Gad, staring at the car key, trying to turn it or melt it, to allow whatever had happened with the gun to happen once again.

"For one thing, you're telekinetic. You can move objects without touching them. Were I to beam what you did with that gun, I'd have a potent force indeed."

Oliver frowns. "Beam? On television?"

"Not quite. I'd have you beam the thought into a transmitter which not only could step up the energy potential of the thought but also could be trained in the direction, say, of the Winfrith Arsenal. You'd have set all guns to spinning."

Gad shakes his head worriedly. The road is thick with mist and drizzle.

"You're driving too quickly."

"Am I boring you?"

"No, dammit. Decelerate."

Sefer peers ahead, taking his foot off the pedal. Around the corner a farmer is moving across the road with his herd of cattle.

" 'Kyou," Sefer replies briskly.

"If you don't mind, Sefer, I'll drive."

Sefer pulls to the side of the road, the mud slushing and grating against the tires. The farmer, gumbooted, soaking, refuses to acknowledge them. For a brief moment, Gad is filled with envy, then turns to Sefer. The latter is settled comfortably beside him, the pistol across his lap.

"The idea intrigued me several years ago," Sefer continues politely. "This Uri Geller performed several telekinetic experiments on television, in Brazil. At least three hundred young-sters began to repeat the same experiments, and successfully. I was sent to Rio, saw a replay of the broadcast. The arms of my wristwatch snapped."

"Do you believe in what he does? I've never seen him."

Sefer smiles pleasantly, almost captivatingly. "As much as Boulter believes in your ability to buy and sell, I do. Yes."

Gad shakes his head. "But I've heard his effects can be repro-duced by any street magician."

"No, he's real enough. He can change the molecular structure of the hardest substance known to man. That's all bending is, you know, a shift in the structure of things."

Oliver stares ahead silently, contemplating more than the road. "Obviously you're implying that Geller and I share some-thing in common?"

"My guess is that you do. Of course, he claims his ability is derived from extraterrestrial contact. He remains thus a dubi-ous sort of figure, though his ability is *not* assumed. No, I think you differ from Geller in that nobody but Gwyneth and I realize your energy potential."

He turns to Gad casually, stuffed down, still, against the seat, in his corduroy trenchcoat, the gun across his lap.

"Ever been to Prague, Mr. Gad?"

"That's it, then," snorts Oliver. "Perfect material for a spy."

Sefer shakes his head.

"Not of the old cold war variety. We know that the Soviets have not taken lightly what we have long considered the magi-cian's bag of tricks: clairvoyance, clairaudience, telekinesis, as-tral travel. . . ."

A long pause, with Gad's breathing becoming the steady sound of wheels on a rain-wet road. He sets the car on automatic pilot, freeing his mind to drift in the enveloping sea of ideas, Sefer's magical notions, fascinating and totally cracked. Imag-ine Intelligence using funds to study spoon benders! My God, what a country, what a place! If the sun has set on the Empire, pray, Mr. Sefer, let it rise on Boadicea's Astral Plane.

So *that* was the word: *Astral* . . . another level.

Gad thought of something Gwyneth had said when they'd

15

stopped for tea in Sherborne, at that low-ceilinged, smoke-beamed shop filled with insufferable sixth formers:

"You're missing a fine time, Ollie. You're sleeping through life, and you don't even know it. Dreams are one thing; astral travel's another. If you remember your dreams, you'll begin to distinguish the astral travel from the dream. Then you'll know when you're actually out-of-body."

"Out-of-body?"

"Traveling on the Astral. Meeting up with things that go bump in the night."

She had explained the mechanism of this other dimension, had drawn a verbal road map of the Astral. And what had Gad done? Certainly not listened. Watched her eyes instead, the demon-green glow of them, the witch glitter, and how her lips, so full and rich, formed patterns which gave birth to words, and how her hair, freshly washed to the color of a Turner sunrise, coppery gold and strawberry red, hung to her shoulders, nestling softly against the bold lines of her shoulders; how the pink cotton polo sweater softened the colors of her *primavera*. For all her talk of the Astral Plane, she seemed of earth indeed. And he remembered, too, how her eyes stayed open, fixed upon him in his passion for her. That witchy glitter.

She'd led him, then, had been leading him all the time. Even to this, his bust on the ear, his drive to Wales. He should have listened clearly to her; he should have read her clearly then. In all her talk of occult notions, he would have seen her clearly. Damn his ego.

That she loved him he did not know. That he loved her he would not think. And for the caring, few moments shared.

"Gwyneth works for you, then?" he whispers.

"With us," answers Sefer. "Upon occasion. Don't feel betrayed, Oliver. She's been trying to open your eyes for two months. You wouldn't listen."

Oliver says nothing. If Sefer knows so bleeding much, there's nothing more to say.

"Yes, we'll talk more about such things later," says Sefer,

16

reading his silence. "However, Mr. Gad, if you feel betrayed, it's your ego's done it, nothing more. My thought's that Gwyneth's your soulmate, though neither of you knows it yet."

Oliver glances at Sefer. The latter is smiling.

"And the sooner you both realize it, the better."

"Who's *your* soulmate, Sefer?"

"A bitch intriguer named Mireille. Died three hundred years ago," he replies briskly. "In Lyons."

Gad smirks. "Still haven't gotten over the shock?"

"I have, though," says the man. "The problem is, *she* hasn't. If you're attentive, Oliver, you'll find her in the back seat of the car."

Oliver shivers and bears down on the accelerator.

2

Asher Berman, poet and singer, stands before the entrance to Porta Portese, the Roman flea market, holding a string of amber beads and staring absentmindedly ahead. For the past two weeks he had been shifted from Kiev, through Moscow Immigration, then by train to Vienna, stopping every five minutes at some ghastly village "so as not to forget the Mother Country"; shunted through more immigration nonsense in Vienna; finally arriving, at four in the morning, in Termini Station, Rome.

It could have made a wonderful song, thinks Asher. If the West were viewed from the vantage point of a predawn arrival in a train station, it would be the perfect advertisement for capitalism, paid by the Marxist publicists: Algerian muggers, homosexual whores, contraband cigarettes, and you clutching at your bowels, though the knife's in your back and the Roman sun is starting to rise. . . .

Asher's uncle, the indefatigable Kolya, hands him several strips of Russian coral to sell and whispers, *"Trantuh myiluh leereh,"* as if it were the password to the Godhead. Holding up his fingers, three, a zero, and *myiluh,* a thousand, thirty thousand . . . coral to sell. Russian coral.

Asher grins broadly, his own prepogrom smile. Kolya pretends not to recognize it, for it seems to imply five thousand years of history, much of it rotten. Kolya had heard his nephew perform once, at a students' club in Moscow, and decided he did not like him at all.

"Let's talk about Jews," Asher had begun, the young man spotlit, his guitar hanging like a growth on his chest. And the students started to laugh. (Kolya misinterpreted the laughter, for what Asher implied was "Let's look at you Gentiles," and the students sensed it, the minstrel-clown setting them up.)

"Jews, as we know, are the smartest people in the world." (Two chords, *Chto mnye gorye!* "What do I care?") "Should I mention their names? Marx, Freud, Einstein. The modern world revolves around these men. . . . And are *we* paying for it!" (A quick chorus of "Eli Eli.") "The Jew can't help himself. Every time he tries to speed the Gentile along the evolutionary road, up pops an Einstein, and suddenly the Jew, who should have said, 'Einstein? Weak in Marxist theory!,' *has* to say, is *compelled* to say, 'Yes, he's one of ours. And how is *yours?*' A mistake. A tactical error. Better to have said, 'Which Einstein are you talking about? The agrarian reformer from Sochi or my wife's brother, the failed violinist?' "

The students were roaring. Kolya had turned red, hating this thin, dangerous, dark-haired and sad-eyed beanpole of a nephew who stood in the center of the light, arms outspread, shrugging.

"Personally, I never cared for this Einstein. His head was always in the clouds. Give me a racing-car driver, a man of the people like our Leonid. 'Relativity, *feh!* Can it beat a 1964 Lotus Racer?' " Shocked silence, then uproarious laughter. And it was Kolya who first had spotted the three KGB men seated at the rear of the café, unmoved and not amused. He had even tried to signal Asher, but the young man was too involved in his own words to sense them as knots on the rope of the hangman.

"I'm crazy," Asher continued. "Forgive me. A typical Jew. Forgive me, students, lovers of learning. Before I break into

19

song"—here his legs wobbled, his arms grew palsied—"let me tell you of the ultimate folly of the Jew in Russia." Long pause. Then, simply: "Isn't *that* the ultimate folly?"

Scattered laughter, then applause.

"But we're here, so why not enjoy it? Waiting like children for the next war. But it will be different. Very different. WORLD WAR THREE, THAT'S FOR ME!"

The song began, with students applauding, then being shhh'd by those who knew that Asher's bullets were lyrics and lyrical.

It was the three drab-looking, humorless KGB men who put a stop to the bullets, letting Asher continue his song in the silence of their office.

No, he had *not* applied to emigrate. He did not *wish* to emigrate.

Kolya, his mother's brother, Kolya's entire family, ecstatically religious, painfully unpragmatic, *had* applied. For three years they had waited. Until Asher had begun to sing.

The irony of the situation, which the young man had pointed out to the officials artfully and unsuccessfully, was that he *liked* the country. He *liked* Russia. It was the fruit of his chaotic orchard. What would his songs mean elsewhere? Wasn't he an artist and, therefore, one born to bite the hand, any hand, proffered in friendship? It was his duty as an artist to tell the world it was crazy. What better place than in Russia to begin the tale?

And yet the brilliance of the government's counterargument was most convincing. Something about his rapport with an audience, his sense of timing, his feeling, his knowing how to set up a bomb, then to explode it. . . . And how did he know about World War III? *"Where the product of the mind is energy?"* It was suggested that Asher spend one month's vacation in Prague to consider the offer while he considered the question, all expenses paid, at the Tesla Institute. Under the direction of Dr. Jira, a most attractive, intelligent and congenial woman.

If the good doctor agreed, Asher would be sent away with Kolya and family. After all, it was what the family wanted.

What had been done to Asher Berman at the Tesla Institute? Experiments in psychic powers, long and boring. Dr. Jira had proved to be better than the description given by Asher's mentors. Though in her early forties, she was slim, with wonderfully wide and deep blue eyes, intelligent eyes, humorous eyes; it was as if the doctor could sense Asher's feeling for a laugh before he actually found an opening. Her mouth was rich and full, and she had a curious habit of running her tongue about her lips. Her hair was deep blond, almost ashen. Like her eyes, it changed in the light and seemed to mirror Asher's moods.

Oddly, he hadn't minded the time she had slapped him when he refused to climb onto the table while she measured something with a strange machine. She had two young assistants, two girls, and when they told him to climb onto the bed, he had said something innocuous: "Well, and has the Prague Spring become a summer festival?" and she had hit him. That evening, while they played chess together, she apologized.

What made the affair even more peculiar was that after two days of experiments he felt as if they were lovers. He wouldn't have minded making an approach. On the fourth day he was about to say something to her when the KGB men returned and told Dr. Jira that Asher Berman was to leave. Immediately.

She was furious. There hadn't been enough time. She couldn't let him go. He'd overheard phrases like "energy potential," "radiational patterns," "absorption on the beta field"; he hadn't the slightest idea what she was saying, but orders were orders, and he was told to pack.

As a gift, Dr. Jira gave him a copper bracelet with an attractive crystal in the center. She also gave him a kiss, to which he responded with more than satisfactory aplomb. Jira was surprised. In microseconds her eyes registered failed possibilities. How very Czech!

"I adore your mouth," he said, and returned to Russia, where he and Kolya and Kolya's own family were given exit visas and sent to the West.

And now in Rome on a Sunday morning, Asher stands at the corner of Viale Trastevere, the sad-looking strings of coral in his hand, reciting to imaginary audiences.

Kolya jostles him, nodding angrily toward a potential customer. Immediately Asher holds up his hand. "Eight thousand Polish zlotys," he declaims in an English learned from nights spent listening to Voice of America. "Failing that, one American dollar or a pair of blue jeans!"

Furious, Kolya begins to harangue him, but it is as if someone, a comic demon, has turned off the sound. Asher's ears start to ring, then whine like a high-power dentist's drill, growing in pitch and intensity. He clutches at his ears and begins to shout. And in the midst of his pain, he feels his wrist burning.

A crowd has gathered. Asher stares uselessly at the faces of all who can do nothing to help. He will die here. He knows it. The stupidity, the uselessness, the burning, and God, the pain. . . .

Then it is over.

Someone offers him a cigarette. Someone hands him a bottle of brandy.

"Grazie," he says politely, his only other Italian phrase besides *trantuh milya lyeereh.* . . ."

"Russo," someone whispers. *"Ebreo.* . . ."

And they continue to stare at him as if he were a five-legged puppy in a pet shop display.

3

Gwyneth Powys is waiting impatiently at the gate, with a kind of masochistic pleasure, as the car pulls into the lane between two broken-down stone walls. With the farmhouse behind her, the mottled Friesian cattle lolling in the dripping fields, one would never suspect the cottage to be anything else but a functioning farm.

Oliver hadn't looked at her as he passed, and this had caused Gwyneth to smile. Replacing the chain, she follows the auto, her gum boots squishing in the thick coffee-ground puddles.

Poor Ollie, she thinks. He's set for an adventure, and his outward docility is fooling no one.

The farmhouse is simple, clean, with an oak table, four chairs, nothing inside to distinguish it from any other farm in the area. If, for whatever the reason, it were to be raided, nothing would be found but a pack of cards, some pencils, a writing tablet. To Gad's ego, it is an embarrassment, for the farm is not even theatrically seedy.

"Would you care for tea, Mr. Gad?" asks Sefer, but Gad shakes his head.

"I'll make us coffee," says Gwyneth, keeping the connection between them alive.

"What, no kiss?" Gad asks, yet turns away as Gwyneth stoops to his level.

A packet of cards, shuffled. And three rows dealt facedown of three cards each.

"Place your right hand over the first card at the top on your left. What number do you feel?"

"Nothing."

"Stop it, Oliver. Relax your hand. A number should pop—"

"Five of spades."

"Gwyneth? Note it on the tablet. Any other fives in that row?"

"No."

"The other rows?"

"Third from the right. Bottom row. I think it's of diamonds."

"Good. Now try it with the next card at the top."

"Two of spades."

"Any others?"

"Listen, why not let me give you the order of *all* the rows?"

Sefer turns with a look of imperceptible surprise toward Gwyneth.

"Please do—"

"Five of spades, two of spades, six of clubs, four of diamonds. Jack of hearts, ace of hearts, seven of spades, ace of clubs. Five of spades."

"You said that."

"Diamonds. Ace of diamonds."

"Right."

They turn over the cards. One hundred percent.

"And how did you know?" asks Sefer coolly.

"I saw it. I concentrated and I saw it. An image popped up."

"Good. Now what's in the other room?"

Oliver closes his eyes. Speaking simply: "Blue wallpaper. A bed. A single bed with a blue-and-white coverlet. A washstand. Two small suitcases, Gwyneth's and mine. . . . I've a headache, Sefer. . . ."

"Look inside your head."

24

"My eyes. It's in my eyes. They must be weary from the road."

"Do you want to sleep?"

"No."

"Why?"

This said, equally simply: "I think I'm rather afraid."

Sefer turns to Gwyneth. "Leave the room, please."

Gwyneth does.

Sefer stares wearily at Oliver Gad. "Here are three cards, facedown. Name them."

Oliver returns his stare, holding his hands above the cards. "Six of clubs. Eight . . . I can't see them. . . . Six of clubs?"

Where did Gwyneth go? thinks Gad.

Sefer smiles slightly, offering an explanation for which Gad secretly had asked. "Some people need generators. They've the power, but they need someone else to boost them. When you concentrated on the cards with Gwyneth in the room, you formed a power link. I hadn't expected this. It will take days, I fear, to build you to the point where you can operate alone."

Oliver starts to laugh.

"You mean I'm a vampire?"

"In a sense. Most people are, to varying degrees. They feed off each other's energy field. Love is a form of vampirism, though one assumes the result to be positive. Analogously, a bloodsucker physically performs what a lover psychically feels. The marriage of the sun and the moon, the moon reflecting the sun's light, the willful give-and-take of it is much the same thing. I hadn't realized, however, the extent of your affect."

Gwyneth returns.

"Here, Ollie."

She removes a ring from her finger, a tiny diamond set within the vines of a gold laurel wreath.

"Hold this in your hand."

Oliver takes it, feels the warmth of it in his palm. Closes his eyes. "Six of clubs . . . eight of spades . . . jack . . . I can't see it. . . ."

25

"Close your eyes and visualize Gwyneth."

Oliver does so. Slowly.

"Queen of diamonds."

Flipping over the cards.

"Good!" Sefer grins, then turns politely to Gwyneth. "Do you mind if he keeps the ring?"

"Ollie would *adore* that," from Gwyneth, laughing.

What they are trying to do, Sefer and Gwyneth, is to make Oliver fully conscious and in control of his powers, like an instrument; to regain the open and spontaneous response of a child; then to control the child's murderous impulses, or at least to redirect them to a socially sanctioned definition of murder, one of a thousand sanctions. But for all the glamour of his life, Oliver Gad has a restless nature. And the inner voice is alerting him to the possibility that one day these people must serve *him*. Even this charming thought, he recognizes, has its dangers, for it is the thought of an adolescent behind the wheel of a powerful machine.

Sensing this, Sefer says, "You have *one* flaw, Oliver, and that is the superficiality of the choices you feel are available to you. With your 'opening up,' these choices will increase, and in direct proportion to the danger of the situation."

Oliver says nothing. Whatever happens, they're linked to him now, and equally responsible. Proof of the Masters serving the Servant. The feeling's almost pleasurable. He'll have the bastard yet, thank you.

"And since you've need of a booster, you cannot be responsible to yourself alone. Gwyneth must be part of the package. Do you understand?"

Oliver nods, turning to Gwyneth.

"Do *you?*" he asks.

She nods as well.

"You can't possibly know," Sefer replies, "either of you."

Oliver rises, sighing, and takes the coffee cup, spilling what is left into the sink.

"What's the yield, Sefer?"

26

"Sit down," Sefer commands.

Oliver is surprised at his tone, but complies.

"Let's talk about magic for a moment."

"What's magic to do with any of this? I'm not drawn to abracadabra."

Sefer nods, politely. "Forget the ritual language, and concentrate on the ceremony. The act of magic consists of the Mage's linkup of his mind force with those forces above, below, to the right, to the left, within and without himself, for a specific intent. *Intention, Mr. Gad, is all.* Once the linkup has been made, then the Mage draws upon those forces, exceedingly clear in his intent. After all, to draw from the wrong source, and for the wrong reasons, would be to short-circuit his mind. Is that clear?"

Oliver shrugs. "Most. And equally uninteresting."

Sefer turns to Gad, watching him long and hard. "*Your* ability is also intentional, Mr. Gad. Did you consider that? You work with what you have, admittedly from your own materialistic point of view. Limited, at best. If you were a surgeon, you'd probably be damned good. Or a bank robber, for that matter. But you lack scope, Oliver. You lack vision."

"Which is why I need you," Gad drawls ironically.

But Sefer ignores the parry.

"You asked what the yield is, Mr. Gad. Let us substitute *stakes* for *yield.* I fear only one thing: the dreadful outcome of the most silently conducted war in the history of man. An Armageddon more ferocious than all the battles and disasters ever to occur on this planet."

Sefer pauses, toying with his coffee cup, then looks at Oliver Gad.

"Up to this point, we've a slight edge: There do not appear to be conscious Soviet operatives within the West; merely programmed psychics, unconsciously driven tools. Our task is to find them, to deprogram them, or failing that, to eliminate them. Then we must begin to work within the East, either telepathically or physically."

So I am to be a paranormal sleuth, thinks Oliver Gad. Walking into places, turning things around. No guns, no James Bond devices. *Mind,* merely.

"And how am I to do this," asks Oliver, "without arousing suspicion? I am, you know, responsible to quite a few people."

Sefer nods, smiling slightly. "The sign of a successful executive, Mr. Gad, is the ability to delegate authority. Consider the possibility of expanding the Consortium to include Middle Eastern, Canadian and American branches. You've merely to 'suggest' the idea to Boulter before you actually suggest it to him. You *do* have that ability, though you don't recognize it."

Oliver turns to Gwyneth. "And I thought it was my charm."

"Let's not be clownish," Sefer interrupts. "I don't wish to pontificate, but this *is* a new phase in the evolution of mankind. You might just be able to help write the rules."

Or to play Faust to your Satan? thinks Oliver. To recite or, better—since he knows Sefer is correct—to become the Undeveloped Unknown, plunging over the Abyss of the Unexplainable?

"Then I know we must fail," says Oliver Gad, grinning. "Let's begin at once."

Unsettling Sefer.

Unsettling them all.

4

Signor Todi, the chief officer of the International Refugee Committee, does not like Asher Berman.

After two hours of disappointing discussions with the young man in that stiflingly close apartment on the Via dei Serpenti, he can think of no other appeal to the fellow's good sense. Every time he mentions emigration to Israel, Berman crosses himself, rolls his eyes and cries, *"Madonna! Mamma mia!"*—a gesture as rude as it is embarrassing.

"How could I be a minority in Israel?"

The uncle, Kolya, slams his fist upon the table with such force that even Asher is surprised.

"Israel has a strong Communist party. You can still be a Communist in Israel," cries Kolya.

"Being a Communist in Israel is like being a dinosaur in Kiev," Asher begins, to an imagined crowd. "Impressive, interesting and an eyesore."

Signor Todi allows himself one irony. "Would you prefer to emigrate to Saudi Arabia?"

Asher Berman thinks for a while, quite seriously.

"If I can be assured of an international harem and an oil well or two." Almost to himself: "If only to free the harem and to blow up the oil well. You don't seem to understand,

29

Signor Todi. I didn't want to leave Russia. The thought of emigrating to Canada is boring, or to the United States. . . ."

For an odd reason, Signor Todi finds himself smiling. Asher doesn't notice this, but Kolya feels it is the final exasperation of a patient, though extremely harried, man. Todi says, *"You do not wish to emigrate to Israel because you are afraid."*

Kolya looks up. The single quality he would never have accused Asher of was fear.

Simply, from his nephew: "Yes. I am terrified."

Now Kolya watches Asher, and the hatred he had felt dissolves into almost paternal compassion. He is, after all, a young man, his comedy nothing but an inner monologue of youthful complaint and worldly contradiction, verbalized for others. Of course, he is frightened. He has every right to be frightened.

"Asher," he says quietly, almost soothingly. Berman turns to his uncle, his eyes moist, lips set tightly in a desperate attempt to control himself. "I am sixty-two years old. So is your aunt. How do we feel? Can we learn modern Hebrew at our age? Can we begin a new work? What does your aunt know about shopping for food, of running a household in a desert country? At least you're young, you've a chance. . . . To us, it's an idea. . . ."

Asher massages his wrist, for it is aching still. He sighs long, bellowslike, and stares at the table. The face of Dr. Jira appears among the teacups; the honey pot is on a table in a room of the Tesla Institute. Asher closes his eyes.

Jira has such a sweet face: such wonderful lines between mouth and nose; clear and soft blue-gray eyes; and her kiss held such promise. . . .

He opens his eyes, looks about worriedly and begins to collect himself.

"Israel," he whispers. "Do you think we're being allowed to go there to be blown up with the world's supply of camels?" Proclaiming: "The World Wildlife Fund regrets to announce the disappearance of two more endangered species: the African Camel and the Soviet Jew, *Meshuganus sovieticus. . . !*"

Signor Todi has to smile, sensing victory. One less tormented refugee to deal with.

"But Jewish girls don't screw," says Asher, fully recovered. "How many *shiksas* can I find in Israel? Who will comfort me in my desperation? Who will consider me a conquest? Maybe I ought to go to Canada. No, that's ridiculous. My closest friend lives in Montreal. I taught him everything I know. He's probably cornered the market on *shiksas.*"

He shrugs. "I am very frightened."

Signor Todi shakes his head. "Not every woman in Israel is Jewish."

Asher snorts. "Not every Italian is Catholic either, but if you think the Church is invisible here, and that it doesn't exercise a psychic spell over even the Italian Communist party. . . ."

Psychic spell. Two months ago Asher would never have used the phrase, more, conceived of it. Two months ago, for that matter, he would never have stopped mid-sentence.

"Do you mind if I go out? Give me an hour, Uncle. . . . Then I'll see. . . ."

Kolya merely shrugs.

Asher Berman takes a bus to Piazza Venezia without knowing why. From there he walks up the steps to the Campidoglio, then beyond the square, without so much as a nod to Marcus Aurelius or to the bird perched between the ears of the philosopher-king's horse. He continues to move through the evening's light mist, the heavy descending air, and finds himself on an embankment above the ancient Senate floor.

It makes no sense, he thinks. Those marble bones before me are History's pickings. And yet Israel. . . . Israel is alive. Why do the Jews require a parallel but separate History? Why couldn't the Jew die on the Senate floor like a Caesar? Why has he refused to accept another's History? Or to see himself as full participant in the West?

Israel is forcing Asher into some kind of decision about himself and about his comedy; it is pushing him off the stage and into the audience along with everybody else. Israel is a commitment he'd not been willing to make—not the physical *aliyah*, return to the homeland, but the metaphysical one, the Israel of his soul.

The Roman twilight, a deep, electrical gray-blue made more profound by the watery air, seems to him to contain his struggle in its ether, to reflect an eternity of bitter choices now judged in bits of broken marble, in crumbling temples propped up with shield and wire. The Roman Senate, ivory-damp, vague in the wet and hazy evening, seems to underline the doubts of his question.

If we are the hope of mankind, the jagged ruins seem to sing, then Israel is our conscience. Our hopes may be dead or dying, but our conscience remains.

It's more than that, thinks Asher. Moral laws change. How can conscience remain an eternal vessel, altering in shape as societies alter, and yet in itself be fixed, immutable?

If I go to Israel—and he knows now he is going—I mustn't go as a Jew. I must become invisible, alien, uninvolved. If I am to learn what this exile means, and what my own role is in Israel's destiny, then I must feel no pull in the heart. I must not go as a Jew. I must go as—yes!—the man in the moon. Or the keeper of Saturn's rings.

Asher's decision to become an extraterrestrial observer in Israel interests him greatly. It is clever. Wise. Filled with intellectual possibilities. Asher Berman in Israel, an interplanetary spy.

"Fascinating," he whispers.

"Canny," he exults.

Then, thinking glumly: Jewish.

5

The results of Oliver Gad's bag of tricks, practiced on a lonely weekend in Wales and threatening nothing so far but the quickening yeast of his boredom:

Telekinesis	—the ability to move objects by an act of will;
ESP	—the ability to divine the thought forms of another person;
Clairaudience	—the ability to hear distant conversations;
Clairvoyance	—the ability to see into the future;
Situational clairvoyance-clairaudience	—whereby the operator creates a thought form of another person or persons, and watches them engage in discourse, and on a subject of his own choosing, then examines their chosen options;
Radiesthesia	—the ability to use a pendulum, divining rod or other dowsing equipment to locate water, missing persons, lost objects, etc., either in the field or over a map. (In this case, Gad's own hand serving as a pendulum.)

33

The results, according to Sefer:

In Gwyneth's presence		In Gwyneth's absence	
a. TK	= 85%	a. TK	= 82%
b. ESP	= 92%	b. ESP	= 78%
c. CA	= 72%	c. CA	= 60%
d. CV	= 78%	d. CV	= 65%
e. SIT-CA-CV	= 59%	e. SIT-CA-CV = 45%	
f. RAD	= 94%	f. RAD	= 94%

His strengths, telekinetic and radiesthetic, had been developed in spite of Gwyneth. His ESP performance fluctuated because of his boredom and, let us admit, his lack of imagination. This was a monstrous assault upon Ollie's ego, for he was quite naturally ready to believe City gossip, "devilishly clever is Gad," "quick to pursue the imaginative lead," *ad nauseam*.

"No," Sefer begins. "I'm afraid you have a barren fantasy life. I wouldn't go so far as to say that you are dull, but the publicity surrounding you unfortunately is much richer than your person."

Gad says nothing, merely toys with Gwyneth's quartz crystal pendulum on the kitchen table, letting it create rainbow patterns on the linen, swarms of blue motes, yellow flies, green and burgundy sun rings sparkling about the room, dissolving to further corners.

"What about trying him in an out-of-body experiment?" asks Gwyneth.

Sefer shakes his head. "Not yet."

"Perhaps something's blocking him out-of-body. We could send him up to find out."

"You've been sending me up enough, thanks," says Gad, flipping the string of the pendulum around his fingers until the crystal is locked in his palm. Warm. Tingling. Suddenly the room grows still. Sound fades away.

"Hello?" asks Gad. "I'd swear this rock was speaking. . . ."

He closes his eyes, shutting them hard. It's not a word he hears so much as a feeling in his gut, a sound in his gut, welling up low and warm. Unbearably sad.

Sefer and Gwyneth watch him, the former surprised to see the tears dripping down the young man's cheeks.

"What is it?" Sefer asks. But Gwyneth puts a hand to his arm.

The rational part of Oliver Gad is fighting for domination.

You're going mad, Ollie, stop being such a clown. Rocks speak only to poets. You're a man of finance! Remember: everything that can be quantified exists. Everything that can't be quantified doesn't.

Then why the tears?

You're tired.

This quartz is humming, working. I can hear it.

Everything possesses a physical law. Though the law's not yet defined, it exists. Give me time, I'll explain everything.

You live for explanations, you bleeding tyrant.

Because you need them. Otherwise, you're nothing but animal instinct. In which case you might as well talk to rocks. You deserve each other.

You're a moralist.

And if you wish to remain an animal, I'll leave you to it. Forewarned, though.

What is the physical law that causes rocks to sing?

They don't sing.

What am I hearing?

I don't know what you're hearing, fool.

A steady hum, very low, very rich. And it is coming from the quartz.

(Reason is silent. Reason is sulking. Reason, to assert itself, is playing for time.)

Oliver opens his eyes to stare at Gwyneth. Her presence alone, her soft summer warmth, is a defiance of thought.

"Ollie," she whispers, and puts her hand over the stone, on his palm. "The next time you step on grass, say, 'Excuse me.'"

Gad does not reply.

Someone's removed the earth, sent Gad spinning. And he

notes, as Reason is jettisoned like the first stages of a rocket, *nothing hurts at all.*

The witchy look in Gwyneth's lime-green eyes, he sees it now as visionary, how she peers through the shadowy glade-glitter, her elfin sexuality, her bardic boldness of speech. There's more to his Gwyneth than he'd ever imagined. Her eyes look upon snow and perceive North Kings in crystal; upon the flames of the fireplace and attract amoral sylphs.

And knowing that everything is alive with Spirit, that Spirit is all, Gwyneth sees Gad's struggle as a spider's web of options, in which he himself is as much the spider as the fly.

The Gwyneth of his weekends, the Gwyneth of the Dorset cottage, exists no more. And both of them know it.

In her arms (how light she is, her butterfly movements, her glade to explore, deeper than he'd ever known—how stupid, Gad, how foolish!), he asks, "When you go to woods, what do you hear?"

"I hear my needs. . . ."

"Your forest friends," he smiles, for the saying of it.

"Ollie, Ollie, if you ever work with Elementals, you'll find they have a different morality. I love their enthusiasm, though I'd never ask for their friendship. Were the Devil to smile at them, they'd as easily smile back. It's all movement for them, it's all flux. Never forget it."

Oliver considers this.

"Does Sefer know you've the witches' art?"

(For Oliver fears it's art, now. He respects it highly. More, he dreads it.) Gwyneth smiles at him, eyes as open and knowing as a child's.

"He tolerates me well enough." She pauses, gazing into the flames. Gad runs his hand along the smooth sharp curve of her cheek, the marble hardness of it; he moves back a strand of her coppery hair, the hard and the soft of her.

"I'm in it for a different reason, though," she whispers, almost to herself.

"And what is that, then?"

Gwyneth pauses, moving her hand beneath the sheets, toying with Oliver.

"There's a rich feminine side to all this manipulation. You'll get killed for it, too, Ollie, if you're not careful. Sefer desperately wants to believe the Feminine's only theory. But I know all about his soulmate, Mireille. She confounds him. She watches him always. She shatters the argument."

Oliver is surprised.

"Mireille? You mean that French girl, the one who died three hundred years ago? You mean she actually exists?"

Gwyneth nods.

"Sefer's so myopic, he thinks she's hovering about him because she's jealous. The truth is she can't move on till his work's finished."

Oliver shakes his head merrily.

"I know *nothing*," he asserts.

Gwyneth does not reply.

But in her silence, contradiction.

Oliver embraces Gwyneth once more, cutting contact with her eyes, wondering whether the Gwyneth he knew before had been more appealing, more *fun*.

Later Oliver whispers, "Did you know you were a generator for me?"

Gwyneth rolls against his shoulder, yawning. "Hmmh?"

"That I perform better with you than without you?"

"What is the schoolboys' word for autoperformance?"

Oliver smiles. "Masturbation."

Gwyneth smiles. "Of course I knew . . . but it works both ways. Remember: What you and Sefer are after doesn't interest me. I've an agreement elsewhere. You're only helping me along. . . ."

"Can you tell me?"

"I've no need yet. I think you'll know. At any rate, my Company prefers silence. One night, perhaps, I'll tell you and you'll regret you ever asked."

Oliver props himself upon an elbow, staring at Gwyneth, emptying himself, waiting for the feeling, letting it flow. He feels her secret, knows it's there, but electric gates spring up to protect her. He starts to climb her psychic fence. A spirit dog barks. He retires, swiftly.

Gwyneth is grinning. "It won't work. Bastard."

Sefer stands before the burgundy Rover. Oddly, Gad's Rolls preens beside it, driven to Wales no doubt by the giant and the dwarf.

Sefer produces three pieces of paper. Before the man can speak, Gad says brightly, "The one in the middle."

"What's written on it?"

"One word: Amsterdam."

Sefer opens the paper, nods.

"Don't tell me, Sefer. I'm going there to investigate chemicals. A merger with Felson's, Hants. Worthy of consideration."

"Good cover. What do you see?"

Gad closes his eyes for a moment, dreamily.

"A bookdealer. Lovely shop, off one of the canals. Soo. Spoo. Something like that. Damn . . . I don't like it."

"What?"

"He's an old Bolshie."

"Was."

"Very religious now."

"Yes."

"He'll be dead within two weeks."

"Possibly."

"But why will I kill him?"

Sefer stares hard at Gad. The question seems more academic than real.

"I don't believe in killing, you know."

Sefer says nothing, turning worriedly to Gwyneth.

"Don't be ridiculous," Gwyneth interjects. "You're only seeing an option."

38

But Gad is none too sure. Gwyneth deals with lower forces, with Elementals, she said it herself. How would she know it's an option?

"You're only to go to Mr. Van Kessel's," says Sefer, "and ask if he has a copy of the works of Ficino."

"Who?"

"If he doesn't, tell him that Mr. Sefer is positive he must have them."

"That's all?"

Sefer shrugs. "He may suggest another dealer."

"Does Van Kessel know you?"

"I think not, Mr. Gad."

"Interesting. Then why should I say Mr. Sefer is positive old Van has these Ficinos? He doesn't even know who you are."

"Because only *his* people know about them. Mentioning *my* name will alert him to the fact that there are other people who know about *him.*"

"May I ask a question?"

Sefer smiles. "Mr. Gad, you've already asked two."

"How did you come to know about this fellow?"

"That need not concern you, Mr. Gad. Suffice to say, I was informed by a colleague. We've reason to believe Van Kessel is part of a nasty little chain. We want you to shake the chain."

Gad nods. *That's* what he's after. A network. Very well, then.

"This is Van Kessel's address."

But Gad shakes his head. "Let me find it myself."

"Call me when you return."

"Where?"

"Think."

"I can't. I get nothing."

Sefer smiles. "I will be doing the accounts for a bookdealer named Whitken. His store is in Cecil Court."

"Not under Sefer."

"Why not?"

Gad turns to Gwyneth.

"Coming?"

39

When she shakes her head negatively, he is surprised.

"You'll be gone only two days, Ollie."

A long pause, with so many implications Gad is confused.

Lovely, thinks Gad. On my own, now. The witch. The monster Mage. Lovely.

6

Signor Todi is extremely proud of himself. Everything is going like clockwork. His account in Liechtenstein will soon show the addition of forty-five thousand Swiss francs, a gift from his masters for the knowledge that Asher Berman will soon be arriving in Tel Aviv. No more responsibility for at least two months. And who were the others who netted him ninety thousand?

Twelve-year-old Zilpah Wallinchek, she was the first. Red-haired, freckled, fiery, with those marvelous wolverine cheekbones; then the musical student Joseph Selliger. Both of them, as far as he knows, are now in Jerusalem, waiting dumbly for Asher Berman to enter their lives.

"A potent gestalt," Waldheim had said, "a young biologist, a musician, a poet. And Dr. Jira is fond of them all. Of young Selliger, especially. She told me his Prokofiev First Piano Concerto showed great promise, and his Bartók. For the amusement of the staff he played the sixth book of *Mikrokosmos* as if he had composed it himself! Zilpah, too, is musical in her own way. Always humming. Then, of course, there's the young *cafénik*, the guitar-strumming Berman. The doctor's a bit concerned about *his* programming. Not enough time, she said. But still, she herself is an artist. Less time under her is more

41

than a great deal of time under any other."

Todi had wondered aloud: "What chord will they strike?"

Waldheim laughed. "How do I know? They're Jews, Todi. A Minor, I'd imagine!"

They were spies of some sort, Todi knew, though they gave no appearance of seeming so. Programmed to perform an action he might one day read about in the papers. All that remained for Signor Todi now was to go to the Vatican and to post a letter to Signor Joop Van Kessel, 21 Spuistraat, Amsterdam. Requesting a copy of the complete works of Giordano Bruno, Vico and, of course, Ficino. And who were they? Renaissance Neoplatonists whose works had been consigned to papal flames.

With characteristic fatality, Todi sighs. *"Casca il mondo"*— shaking his head gravely—"the world's falling down," then wondering where that children's jingle originated.

Perhaps he would be surprised to learn that the apocalyptic rhyme came from Cardinal Antonelli's tongue, one hundred-odd years ago, when the statesman had heard of Garibaldi's approach to Rome—an approach that would change his world, his established world, forever.

Had Todi known, in some obscure part of his being, he would have been forewarned.

7

"O liver. My God, man, where are you?"
"On my way to Amsterdam."
"What?"

Gad could imagine Boulter's cheeks quivering with the sort of burlesque rage affected by Robert Morley. Boulter was the only other man who could get away with it.

"I'll tell you when I return. Meanwhile, have a look at Felson's, the chemical firm. I'm going to approach your old boy at the Algemene Bank and see if there's anything in chemicals going begging. Let's splurge for a merge."

"But it's the worst time to consider a merger, Ollie! There isn't a firm hasn't hit the bottom."

"Precisely. Attributable to wrong thinking, Sir Bill."

There is a silence at the other end.

"Will that be all, m'lord?" drawls Boulter with broad sarcasm.

"Not quite. Tell your street urchins to dump the following. Got a pen?"

"Don't be funny."

"I'm not." Gad grins and checks his watch for the proper time. Though he enjoys the fight, he doesn't want to miss the flight.

"Sell *all* gilts."

43

"What?"

"Don't fret, Sir Bill. It's only three and a half million pounds. Also Amos Whitbread, Jackcheap's, Harbinger Coke & Nickel, Rod Arrow and Colson Sidearms. That should bring us up to seven mill— let's see. . . . Need two more."

Gad places his hand over the buff salmon back page of the *Financial Times*, letting it play over the columns of equities, waiting for the sensory neurons to connect with a losing enterprise.

"Whoops. How much do we have in Malay Tin?"

"Approximately four hundred thousand pounds. . . ."

"Not worth the bother."

"Ollie, are you sure you must go to Amsterdam?"

"Absolutely. Don't fret. I'll be back in a day or so. You've enough to do without me. And here we are: Blivens Enterprises—poor Sir Michael, he'll ride you when you've dumped his shares, especially since his company just went one-for-three for my benefit. And a good-bye to . . . Ewell Glade Industries."

"What?"

"That makes it an even nine. All of which should be invested in the following three minor industrials: Copley of Sussex; De La Ware Radionics; and Magneto-Geometrics, Hants. Make it an even investment, Sir Bill."

"But what do they do? Has Research—"

"None of them has any financial strength at the moment."

"Mr. Gad . . . !"

"Not to worry. We'll enter the elevator in the basement, emerge at the ninth floor. Hang onto Copley for three years, De La Ware for six and Magneto for nine months. Simple arithmetic, Sir Bill."

"But what do they *do?*"

Gad looks up at the flightboard as the hostess calls for first boarding on KLM 273 to Amsterdam.

"Sorry, Sir Bill. *Must* dash."

"Mr. Gad, this is the most outrageous exercise!"

"Repeat all your thoughts when I take you over the top—

at roughly, say, one hundred and twenty million? Toodle-oo. . . ."

Gad puts down the receiver, grabs the leather bag at his feet, moves smoothly down the corridor at Heathrow to the flight officer.

He stops himself from considering the possibilities of his transaction. A major upset in the Consortium. Boulter answering hundreds of questions from his investors. Within three hours the Press on his back. Research discovering that Copley, De La Ware and Magneto construct machines which nobody but a magician could understand. But we are entering the Age of Magic, are we not?

"And is the world ready for me?" Gad whispers, grinning, and hands his boarding pass to the Beatle-banged blond stewardess. "Being that I am more than ready for the world?"

The thought of Boulter and the Consortium's dumping nearly half their shares on his advice—and oh, the nature of that advice!—makes Oliver laugh.

It's nice, he thinks, to be only thirty-six.

8

Sefer comes up from the tube at Leicester Square and gazes about. The drizzle has thickened to fog, transforming the drifting passersby to thin steaming cattle in vague and yellow pools of light. Wrapping his mac tighter about him and opening his umbrella with a quick and practiced snap at the brace, Sefer moves into the mist, one more gray and chartered accountant in a gray, depressing town.

He waits for the light at Charing Cross, eyes lowered, head down, then moves before the fume-belching buses. An actor, standing at the Aldwych main door with overemphatic boredom, eyebrow cocked, head swiveling to gain unconscious applause, booms: "They've locked the bloody theater on me." (That "bloody" makes him a declared prole, thinks Sefer. Democracy in the stalls.)

Sefer turns into Cecil Court, the cozy alleyway of bookshops and print stores, pausing before a shop called IMAGES. He stares at a display of Oxford University Press books, losing himself for a time in the titles. The *Dictionary of the Christian Church* particularly holds him, but the price, eighteen quid, somewhat dulls his curiosity. Christianity has always puzzled him. Christ himself was an enigma, though the historical Jesus was absurdly comprehensible. The mystery for me has always been the Resurrection, but Crucifixion is humanity's game.

He sighs, reaching into his pocket. He'd a tenner, two fives. . . .

Sefer enters the bookshop, preparing to live on chips for the week. Then a whimsical notion overcomes him.

"Good afternoon," he tells the manager. "I'd like to purchase that dictionary in the window."

"Very good, sir. It's a reprint, you know. Been out of stock for nearly twenty years."

"Could you send the bill to my office?"

For a fraction of a second the manager pauses, then nods. "Certainly. The address?"

Sefer pulls a card from his wallet. The manager nods once again as Sefer writes his name atop the card. Let them pay for my pleasure, he thinks, imagining Whitehall accountants scratching their less-than-magnanimous heads over the entry: eighteen pounds for a Christian dictionary?

Sefer thanks the manager and leaves the shop, crossing the alleyway.

At Whitken's Bookshop, Sefer moves quickly to the room at the rear, opening his briefcase. But not before Julian Webster, the mystic gourmand, has spotted the Oxford volume.

"What's this?" he yells, his myopic eyes bullfrogging below the shock of violent red hair. "O.U.P.'s *Christian Dic?*"

"A reissue."

"Marvelous! Why don't we have it?"

"I wouldn't know."

Julian sighs, raising his eyes skyward. "Sarah, our twitty manageress, been moving too heavily into Wolfbane, that's why."

Flinging his arms toward a counter: "Look at this: shelves of magical unguents and bronze pentacles—no doubt made in Taiwan."

Sefer turns to the rear shelf, staring at the vials of oils and perfumes, sorcery's paraphernalia. He feels an idea beginning to form. This happens every time he speaks with Julian. In a way Gad is Julian Webster's idea, for associations pop from

47

the celibate Webster as easily as bubbles from the mouth of a frog—strange connections, occasionally tantalizing, often murky.

When the psychic branch had begun to sprout a limb, Sefer had gone to Whitken's to purchase some materials on the paranormal. Julian had helped him to several works in the field, dancing about each volume with the authority of Baryshnikov. A rich mine, saw Sefer at once. (God bless England; how it produced these unknown and eccentric authorities in droves!)

Webster had asked what Sefer did for a living—"Accountant," he had replied, automatically. The rest was diplomatic gamesmanship, as natural to Sefer as the genealogy of Isis was to Julian Webster.

Without Julian's awareness, Sefer had begun to mine him to his rich and occult depths. Webster, as it turned out, was also Gwyneth Powys's first cousin.

"Along comes the *Christian Dic*, right under our nose," Webster grieves, "and we miss it!"

"There's a display in the windows of IMAGES."

But by now, uncaring, Webster is leafing rapidly through the volume. "Look at this. Giving Julian of Norwich her due, the cunt. . . . 'Unction,' a nice little entry. The Roman Catholics certainly preempted our Sarah the Manageress and her magical unguents, I must say."

"What do you mean?"

Julian looks up, as if the statement required no explanation. "All the Old Church business, the rites, the language, the oils, drawing the divine to the human—it's just the old *Abra* made Official. The Mage as Pope."

Then, sotto voce: "Something no knowledgeable Mage would ever wish to be. . . ." Sighing, "Well, here's your book. What's this?" Webster stares at Sefer appraisingly. "*Eighteen quid?* That's stiff for an accountant. Why'd you buy it?"

Sefer smiles politely. "What makes you think I did?"

"You certainly didn't steal it."

Frowning now, expecting to see Sefer's sitting room filled

with volumes lifted from Whitken's itself.

"It's for my nephew," Sefer explains. "He's reading Classics."

"Oh? Greek or Latin?"

"Welsh," says Sefer dismissively, putting the book into his briefcase and pulling out the accounts receipts.

Magical oils. Unguents. The words meant something to Sefer; there was some connection between the words and his present adventure. No forcing the connection, however: no need. He'd wait for the connection to pop, for pop it would.

"Mr. Webster?" Sefer calls. "What are those unguents supposed to do?"

"Same thing as baptism: keep you open to the touch of spirit."

" 'Kyou," Sefer replies, as if the information were infinitely more complex than the quantum theory and far beyond the intelligence of a simple accountant.

Then the pop occurs, in the toss-off of Webster's phrase: *"Open to the touch."*

So. One needn't be brainwashed at all. One merely had to be open to the touch. Find a young sensitive. Open him. Touch. But there's more. . . .

Sefer thinks: I perform Deed X upon my subject. I give him something which he will associate with Deed X. An unguent. A gift. If he is open to the touch, he will do whatever Deed X requires *whenever he wears the unguent* or *whenever the "gift" is activated.*

Webster's correct, once again.

There *is* marvelous magic in the Church. More than eighteen quid's worth. . . .

Pop pop!

9

It is not only the waters of Amsterdam, the ever-shifting play of light and mist upon its face, the singular breaking up of a transparent plane of land by canal and boat; it is the sky, the size of it accentuated by the startling flatness of the land, spraying the scape with light as thin as it is vast.

Gad likes the city immediately. There is a feisty directness about it, and a sensuality odd for a northern city. The people look you in the face, take your measure, gull you cockily. Rude they are, and fresh.

He wants to check into a hotel; the Red Lion looks Gothically anonymous, off the Dam, beyond the pigeons and the trippers taking the slow route to the opium dens of Nepal. Three blocks, he senses, from the whores.

No, he thinks.

Do the job first.

Besides, he'd have to deal with his man at the Algemene Bank, Mousie, or whatever he was called. Chemicals, fertilizers. Even if Ollie returns to London with nothing but a prospectus, it is ample cover. He'd check into the hotel later. He'd see the whores.

The city would be floating still—crystallike and pure—were it not for Progress in the guise of macadam. The Spui, a conjunction of several of the major water networks, had been paved over for trams. A pity, too, since the houses which lined the street were some of the most burgherish and imposing, yet now had become thoroughly out-of-scale, lost in the street traffic.

But still there are bookshops on every corner, ancient, crusty books, stamps and antiques stores, and all so very comfortable. . . . Gad, strolling along the Spui, even fancies himself as a burgher: an hour's worth on the old stamp collection, a fair deal for a seventeenth-century Delft vase, two seconds with a woman in a window. The old burgher life, yo-ho-ho. Gad alive. Gad manic. Gad above all.

"Mr. Van Kessel?"

The old man, shaggy-haired, bushy-browed, with an exceptionally bulbous nose, turns from the counter to the young and hyper man at the doorway.

"Hello hello hello."

Van Kessel says nothing. Does nothing. Waits.

"Would you be shocked to learn I flew here from England. . . ." Van Kessel does not reply. "Simply to see you?"

Van Kessel smiles almost shyly. Still says nothing. Gad frowns. "Do you speak English?"

Van Kessel nods. "Of course I do." Almost rudely. Assertively.

"But you're not surprised."

The eyebrows rise.

"The truth of the matter is, my friend, I've come to see you about a Ficino."

Van Kessel raises his eyebrows even further.

"Do you have the complete works? Let's not waste time, Mr. V. Our mutual friend Sefer says you're the best, when it comes to Ficino."

Van Kessel mutters to himself. His eyes appear to water. He reaches toward a cabinet beneath a shelf of books. Oliver moves forward, grabbing the man by the arm.

51

"I want that book *now*. . . ."

"It has gone," Van Kessel replies flatly.

"Where?"

This said as a light bulb actually shatters within a Liberty-style lamp on the old man's desk. Van Kessel is startled and turns to the lamp.

What's this? thinks Ollie. Did I do that? Why, I did indeed.

Oliver smiles, picking up a letter opener, holding it before Van Kessel's face.

"Watch this, old man; pretend it's your brain."

Slowly the letter opener begins to bend. The bookshelves rattle.

Van Kessel closes his eyes, moving his mouth like a fish. Pale and perspiring.

Oliver raises his hand, solemnly pointing his finger at the bookshelf. Three volumes advance forward like soldiers and fall off the shelves.

"My God," Van Kessel whispers, shaking like a vessel in the Channel.

"The *book*, old man. Where did it go?"

"To Rome . . . I sent it yesterday. . . ."

"To whom?"

Van Kessel points, quivering, toward a paper upon his desk. Oliver snatches it—*Italy*, Sig. *Todi*—then he puts the paper in his pocket, smiles pleasantly and starts for the door. Then he thinks better of it. "How many orders have you received from this man?"

"I . . . I must check my records. . . ."

"Do. . . . I've the time."

Gad closes the door, advancing once again toward the trembling man. Van Kessel moves slowly, jerkily, to his desk and opens a large, tattered gray ledger. His hands are shaking. Moisture has appeared on his upper lip.

"Easy, my friend. I don't want us having to deal with a stroke."

Van Kessel closes the ledger, panting. "There have been

two others. Six weeks ago. And one, the year before . . . that I remember."

"What were the books?"

"Neoplatonists . . . Bruno, Della Mirandola and, of course, Ficino. . . ."

"Is that all you do? Send books?"

Van Kessel looks up, certain the young man is playing with him. Hello, thinks Gad. Won't sly Sef be surprised by the answer?

"I'm afraid I cannot answer that question."

"I am afraid you are correct," says Gad, staring hard at Van Kessel.

The man begins to clutch at his own throat.

"If you need a doctor. . . ."

"Help me," wheezes the man, feeling his glands swell, his larynx collapsing in the happy clutches of a hyped-up ape. How did it happen? How had Oliver Gad given birth to an ape? It was how the man looked, how his fear started him drooling, nostrils flaring. If you need an ape, rumbles Ollie, I'll give you one indeed. The thought had been given force and was now assuming form. Oliver felt the force along his spine; it moved as a prickly wave of heat, emerging as an invisible vapor from his mouth, though he'd felt the form, the rankness of it. Was it bile? he had thought. But his sense range had expanded beyond the normal, and there indeed was the Ape, visible now to Ollie, flinging the terrified old man like a rag doll about the store.

Oliver holds out a hand, and the Ape turns to him, confused.

"What do you do, old man? Hurry!"

Van Kessel shakes his head in terror. Gad himself is feeling dizzy. The Ape stares uncertainly at both men. Who is Master here?

"Tell me!"

"Liechtenstein . . . account of Yesod . . . I transfer funds. . . ."

"Here. . . ."

Gad is worried and unbuttons the man's collar. But the Ape won't let go. Gad is surprised to see Van Kessel's eyes turning upward and a gray bilious fluid pouring from his ears.

"Jesus God," says Ollie, backing up against the door and staring in awe as the bookshop loses its gravitational bearing and all the volumes, lamps and drawers fall, pop, spin, open, crash noisily within a whirlpool of energy, flinging about with a roar and a whoosh!

Gad breathing hard, closing his eyes, whispering, "Jesus God, protect me, Jesus God, protect me. . . ."

The Ape has squashed the man's larynx as if it were a week-old banana. The Ape is now playing hide-and-seek in the book-shop, smashing everything in sight, pulling it all apart.

Gad raises his hand, unconsciously, right hand held high, left to the ground, and the moment slows, connecting with his right arm, then burying itself through his body, shuddering spasmodically, losing itself in the ground. The Ape disappears, hooting elsewhere.

Gad stands by the door of the shop, imagining an invisible wall covering its exterior. Placing a dragon before it. Chaining the dragon to the wall. Good morning, dragon, here's a bone for you, if you're good. . . .

Straightening his tie, patting his hair in place, Mr. Oliver Gad walks toward an electric tram, then decides, for his own sake and everybody else's, to walk instead.

What had happened?

He'd meant only to scare the man, not to kill him. So he had projected an ape, yes, but only because he felt Van Kessel resembled one, the way his mouth was slavering, the way he was snorting. The rest was overkill. Botched up. Stupid, Gad, really stupid.

Then the dragon. If he could project an etheric ape, why not an astral dragon? The sense of it would keep everybody out of the shop until he could leave. The wall would cover it. Nobody would look inside. . . . But what a foul-up!

The only rationalization he could muster for Van Kessel's death was the fact, yes, the certainty, that the man had been engaged in something ferocious.

Well, all right. This Italian writes him for the book. It's a signal, obviously. The man transfers monies to Liechtenstein. *Account: Yesod.* Two transfers in six weeks. One the year before. Interesting, indeed. And so what?

Gad is exhausted. He has no idea where he is walking. The streets mean nothing to him now. Amsterdam is a mist, mind's a blur.

Choose the first hotel you see.

No luggage, lost it on the plane.

Up for a kip, thanks. Won't be but an hour.

Send me up two dozen women of the windows, and wake me when it's over.

10

At Ben-Gurion Airport stands the Welcoming Committee in the person of stout citizen Michael Kazin, mathematician from the University of Kiev, a dissident, five years in a *gulag,* said to be one of Solzhenitsyn's composites of Ruben in *The First Circle,* a man accustomed to moving everyone about easily and with good humor; short, stocky, well tanned, an incessant smoker, and deep in the eyes (Asher recognizes it immediately), the *gulag* knowledge still.

Asher refuses to settle with Kolya in the suburbs of Haifa. "I insist upon Jerusalem," he says.

Kazin starts to laugh good-naturedly. *"I've* been insisting upon Jerusalem for eight years myself, Citizen Berman. What else is new?"

But Asher shakes his head. "You don't understand. To be in Israel and not to live in Jerusalem would be like going to Moscow without visiting Lenin's Tomb. God forbid, such a disgrace!"

For a moment Kazin's eyes cloud. Is he joking?

"There are only so many apartments, Mr. Berman."

"It would be like moving to Sochi," the young man continues, "and turning your back on the Black Sea. Horror of horrors! Defiance of defiances!"

Kazin looks at Kolya, who is stamping his feet impatiently. An Israeli girl in uniform calls raucously in Hebrew to Kazin, tossing her head in Asher's direction.

"What did she say?"

Kazin smiles pleasantly. "She said you are a pain in the ass."

Asher returns his smile, winks at the girl.

"Tell her I'm willing to try anything once, if she is."

Kolya blushes. "That's enough!"

And yet Kazin translates. The girl makes another remark.

"She says that since neither she nor you possesses a male organ, would you mind if she uses her rifle?"

Asher claps his hands delightedly, grinning broadly at the girl. "Land of Milk and Honey! Tell her that if she can hold me the way she is holding that rifle, then I'll cough up bullets for the both of us."

Kazin raises his eyebrows, yet duly translates.

"She feels, judging by your tongue, that you've had great practice holding your own rifle, and don't need her. . . ." Taking Asher by the arm and almost whispering conspiratorially: "Come. You'll drive with me to Jerusalem this afternoon."

Asher blows the young girl a kiss. Lest she lose the last line, Girl-soldier curtsies, eyes black and merry.

"Your songs are quite well known here," says Kazin, hailing the beat-up gray Volkswagen bus that is to take the group to Haifa. "But you'll discover the competition is fierce."

Grinning, Asher replies, "I don't know. Perhaps I will play better in Hebrew."

Young, healthy soldiers everywhere, their faces clear reflections of an ancient Europe and troubled Middle East. Asher Berman, exhilarated and confused, is feeling the need to comfort every young woman with apples. Thinking: What was Rome but Babylon? Thinking: The vitality here will require a ferocious "plugging in"—and not of the kind born of loneliness (how another Asher once had slept in the arms of a whore off the Roman *autostrada,* some henna-haired Abruzzi farmgirl seated in a hut, her white linen cloth raised like a Mongol's prayer flag atop a pole). Not here. This is the future in the Immediate, the Now of things made all the more poignant and all the more sexual by the threat of war.

The Union of Mars and Venus, that is Israel.

Wait.

Asher's desire to be lunar is vanishing beneath the Eastern sun: Babylon, Greece, the Song of Solomon—what a rush of history bludgeoning him, swamped in the whirlpool of archetype. Wait. Be patient. The moon has her own laws, her own song to sing.

Let it come.

Asher Berman is deposited at the dormitory section of the Hebrew University, in a quarter whose wing had been damaged the previous week by two anonymous Palestinians with a penchant for blowing up Centers of Learning. Immediately the university students had gone on strike, threatening those students who refused to stand guard duty with expulsion or scrambled brains.

"The university is free to everybody," Kazin explains. "Too often such freedom is taken for granted. The students guard their dorms, but many of the Palestinians have refused to do service—though they share the same classrooms, teachers, laboratories. As a consequence"—he shrugs dryly—"they are not considered potential fund-raising alumni."

Asher smiles, staring at the sand-bagged wing open to the Eastern heavens.

"Was anyone hurt?"

"Naturally. Two Yemenite girls were killed, and one Druze Arab seriously injured."

"Did they catch the Palestinians?"

"One, yes. He's a popular hero among the European Left: a book burner, if ever there was one."

"And the other?"

"Oh, they know who *he* is. A regular guest of the democracy of France. . . . I adore France," says Kazin, opening the door to Berman's next home. Then: "Your roommate. Another Russian."

A tall, thin young man leaps up from his bed: pale, somewhat effete, with long hair and soft brown eyes. His nostrils tip delicately upward. After striding quickly across the room, he takes Asher's hand in his own.

"We met once! Joseph Selliger."

Asher smiles grimly. Damn, a homosexual admirer!

"And where did we meet?"

"Where do you think?"

Asher turns to Kazin, puzzled. Kazin looks down embarrassedly.

"In Prague?" Asher remembers very few in Prague. Only Jira, the good doctor.

"Prague? No, but you were in the audience, somewhere." The young man smiles, pushing aside his hair. "I was performing."

Then Asher remembers.

"Of course. The Bartók! You were quite wonderful. . . . But that *was* in Prague. . . ." Asher senses there is more to this than a casual encounter.

"You're fortunate," says Kazin, yawning, "to have each other for roommates. Tomorrow morning Mrs. Rosen from my office will call you. . . ."

"Not about work?" asks Asher forlornly. "Give me a week to rest."

"No." Kazin laughs. "It's about learning how to talk all over again."

"Hebrew," snorts Selliger, rolling his eyes heavenward. "If our beloved Soviet government only knew what torture it is to learn the language, they'd let *every* Jew emigrate, just for the experience."

Asher smiles, crossing to one of the closets and placing his suitcase within.

"Kazin's leaving," Selliger calls familiarly. Asher turns.

"Thank you," he says, "for translating in the airport."

59

"If you have any problems, ask Mrs. Rosen. . . ."

"She must be God," Asher replies.

"Oh but she's wonderful," Selliger begins, as Kazin leaves. "Anything—"

"Please *gospodin* . . ." interjects Asher, turning from the closet. "I'm exhausted. I don't give a damn about Mrs. Rosen."

Joseph is stunned. Hurt. He shrugs carelessly, massaging his forearm. The gesture is not lost upon Asher.

"Something wrong?"

Joseph Selliger shakes his head. A delicate copper bracelet with a shining crystal gleams on his wrist.

"Sometimes it hurts, that's all."

Asher smiles, holding up his own arm.

Selliger stares. The bracelets are identical.

"What does it mean?" whispers Selliger, and in such awed tones that Asher has to smile.

"It doesn't mean we're married, Joseph. Now let's both sit down. Were you also in love with Dr. Jira?"

"Who?"

"Oh, please, Joseph. . . . The *doctor* in Prague."

Selliger shakes his head confusedly.

"I don't know who you mean. . . . I was never in Prague."

"But I *heard* you in Prague. Isn't Jira the woman who gave you the bracelet?"

"Who?"

And from the look in Joseph's eyes, the startled doelike glance, Asher senses he is not pretending.

The night, he knows, is going to prove uncomfortably long.

11

Everything hurts.

As soon as Gad rolls over on the unfamiliar bed, his hand touching the unfamiliar headboard, he tries to open his eyes, but they appear to be glued shut. His mouth feels like an ashtray. He forces his eyes to open, focusing hard on the room about him, straightening the blurry edges of the nightstand, the stained beige lace curtains.

What time is it? And what has happened?

He rises stiffly, muscles breathing fire. Crossing to the sink and splashing his face with cold water, breathing deeply until his lungs are aching.

Christ, he thinks, I've the flu.

But it isn't the flu, and he knows it. What now? He looks at his watch. Twenty to three. Over an hour late to the meeting at the Algemene Bank Nederland.

He staggers to the phone, keeping his mind focused on the present. He wants out. He wants home:

"Mummy," he whispers, dialing the telephone operator, "you never told me the facts of life. . . ."

"Heer Meeuwse, Leidseplein Branch." Gad giving his apologies, explaining his delay. Gad hoping Meeuwse would meet him in an hour, wherever possible, no, he'd a flight back that evening, impossible to have dinner. . . .

Shivering still, Oliver Gad goes down to the barbershop and asks the young woman to wrap hot and scented towels about his face; to massage his scalp with her knuckles; to perform miracles with her razor.

At the Café Américain, off the Leidseplein, Oliver Gad meets the stocks and shares manager, Heer Meeuwse. The older man, startlingly blond, almost an albino, is nonplussed by the sight of the Silver Fox, the living legend: so young, yet so ancient, something slightly degenerate about the fellow, how close-shaved he appears, and watery-eyed, adolescent and yet de-bauched, resembling one of those decadent English poets.

They sit at a table overlooking the square, their faces lit by a small, fringed Art Deco lamp. Gad stares about him: a few elderly people, but mostly students, intelligentsia, artists.

Meeuwse watches him, sensing his curiosity.

"The Stadschouwburg is across the street," he begins. "The State Theater. Those people are probably from the Dans Thea-ter. Then through the Vondelpark there is the Concertgebouw, our concert hall. Many artists come to this café, after re-hearsals."

"Lovely," Gad replies. A waiter in *frac* appears. Gad orders a hot chocolate, Meeuwse a *genever*.

"I am quite sorry we were unable to see each other this morning, Mr. Gad. I have brought you all the material of ferti-lizer companies in Holland. As you will see, the important Ger-man-Dutch merger, AKZO, is in a critical stage."

"I'm interested in local companies really," says Gad, smiling. "High yield, overestimation on the A'dam exchange. . . ."

"Overestimation?" Meeuwse asks politely.

"On their arse and ready to plunge." Gad grins. "Quick to accept the possibility of economic aid in . . . various forms."

Meeuwse nods politely. "Certainly," thinking: *What a little rat. Coming to A'dam to terrify the natives with his checkbook.*

"May I ask, Mr. Gad: Are you considering a merger?"

"Possibly. Or takeover."

Again, Meeuwse nods politely. "I assume you have a holding company either in Holland or . . . somewhere?"

Gad says nothing, takes the brochures, and his right hand begins to tingle immediately. A hit! A palpable hit! He folds over the flap of the first prospectus, Koningen Elemental, and places the material in his briefcase. The gesture is not lost on the Dutchman.

"What do you think of the situation here?" asks Gad, returning Meeuwse's curious stare.

"Thunder above the lake," Meeuwse replies.

"Meaning?"

"Meaning we Dutch are doing what we've always done: demanding greater social justice while we enrich our own banks. We're a very serviceable country, Mr. Gad. Three hundred years ago, when we were fighting off your invasion, we were also selling you weapons. Liberty and good business, that's Holland."

What rats! thinks Gad.

And they both smile with weary grace, again prepared to dance the Nationalists' Gavotte; failing that, the Chauvinist Minuet.

Before Gad boards the plane to London, he asks many questions about the Dutch attitude to the EEC. A most interesting discussion. Worthy of a page in the *Financial Times*. But Gad is sick and shivering and dares not contemplate the reasons until he is safely in England.

At Heathrow, in the washroom, he nearly passes out from retching.

12

J oseph Selliger says:
    "I must have wanted to emigrate always. At the con-
servatory, every reference to European music was slight-
ing. Brahms was a German nationalist, corrupting the people's
ideal; Mozart was a part of the conspiracy of Freemasonry;
Wagner a Nazi; Mahler, worst of all, a self-dramatizing Jew-
turned-Catholic. Rimsky-Korsakov? Here was a *great!* And
Glinka. The seeds of degenerate individuality were already
planted in Stravinsky's *Sacre.* Prokofiev? Past history. Shostako-
vich? Excellent, especially in his works for the mediocre. Do
you know the humiliation I had to endure because of the success
of *Babi Yar?* 'There, you see?' This from my fellow students.
'Who says the National Conscience does not recognize the Jewish problem? Here you have our leading composer and poet
writing together to portray the Soviet attitude toward the Jewish tragedy.' Excellent, I thought. Dead is dead. What about
the living? What about *us?*"
    He pauses and wipes his brow. He is sweating.
    "I was to perform the First Piano Concerto of Prokofiev. I
played it and won the competition. "Bis! Encore!" I thanked
the judges, told them I refused to play ever again until I'd
been allowed to emigrate to Israel. Mind, I'd never made a

64

political statement in my life. It simply came out, in spite of myself. I was fed up with their hypocrisy! I wasn't like you, Asher. Nobody ever really knew how I felt. And I must say I was miserable, because the government had spent a great deal of money training me. I offered to return their money, with time.

"Nobody at the conservatory would speak with me. I couldn't give a damn. It was out now, in the open. I was sent home and a week later found myself being hustled by two bullies onto a train."

"What is so *extraordinary* about your talent?" asks Asher.

Joseph shrugs. "I have perfect pitch. I can reproduce quarter tones, half tones. If you give me an Indian raga, I can reproduce the tones as well. But so can half a dozen others at the conservatory."

Asher shakes his head. Pitch, combined with an ecstasy or trance state? He remembers Selliger during the Bartók piece. His eyes were open, staring hard, but his gaze did not appear to be fixed on anything. It was as if his mind were elsewhere, his eyes perceiving order, scales, tones from another dimension. He did not sit erectly in the chair. And he held his head cocked at a curious angle. It was most disconcerting.

"And they let you emigrate?"

"Yes."

"And you remembered *me?*"

"Of course. I heard you, twice, at the students' club. My cousin has that record of yours, *Mongolian's Night Out.* I thought it was very funny. I must say, I was surprised to see you in the audience."

Asher frowns. Why has Selliger blocked Prague?

"Who else did you see? When you saw me? Any others now in Israel?"

"A little girl from Leningrad. She was on the plane with me, though we didn't talk."

"And she's here in Jerusalem?"

Joseph shrugs. "I think so, I don't know. . . ."

"What was her name?"

65

"Zilpah something . . . I don't know, really." A bit too casually, "I've never been much of a Don Juan."

Asher smiles warmly. "I'll make it up for the both of us. Tell me, who gave you the bracelet?"

"An admirer. . . . Someone just handed it to me. . . . Before I left. . . ."

Much later, with the lights out, the moon pouring through the window, Asher turns to Joseph lying across from him. He barely can see Selliger's face in the dusky room.

"What did you think of Dr. Jira?" he asks.

"Please . . . I don't know this doctor. You frighten me. You make me believe I should know him."

Asher sits up on the bed, frowning. His voice is tense, yet strained with fatigue. "Listen, why don't we throw these bracelets away?"

"Why? I don't want to."

Asher nods.

"Nor do I," he says. "An admirer. . . ."

"Anyway, why *should* we? For me the bracelet is a victory. A good riddance present."

"Good riddance, that is fine. But who gave it to you?"

Selliger stirs upon the bed, running his hand nervously through his hair.

"What does it matter? I finished a concert, they pressed it upon me."

"What concert?"

"The Bartók, I think it was—"

"I heard you play the Bartók, Joseph. And it was in Prague. And look! I have the same bracelet. *Also* from an admirer! Her name, Joseph, is Jira and she is extremely—"

"Damn you, I don't know Jira! And if I did know her, I wouldn't care! What does it matter? We're also wearing Mogen Davids, the both of us. So what?"

Asher shrugs. "So nobody ever made a religion out of two bracelets, Joseph. The only one who seems to be wanting to start a church is Jira."

Prissily Selliger rises from the bed and crosses to the piano. He stares reflectively at the keyboard. "Did anyone ever give you a gift after you'd performed?"

"Yes. . . ."

"Do you remember every gift ever given to you after a concert?"

"Only of the mermaid variety: half goddess, half fish."

"Be serious. For myself, half the time I'm still so involved in the concert I don't even know my name. . . ."

Asher nods. "True. . . ."

"So how can I remember every gift?"

"But I remember *place*, Joseph. I would know if I've given a recital at the student's club in Moscow or at Tretyakov's in Kiev. And I would certainly know if I gave a concert in a foreign country."

Joseph slams his hands upon the keyboard, gritting his teeth. "I was never in Prague, I was never in Prague, never in Prague!"

Asher starts to laugh nervously. "Here, you needn't shout. Maybe I'm just being paranoid."

"We're not in Russia, you know. You can drop the paranoia."

"Hard to rid yourself of old habits."

"I don't want to hear any more about those bracelets. . . ."

Asher nods, yawning.

"Relax, Joseph. It was just a coincidence. Leave it at that."

Well, I know *I* was in Prague, thinks Asher, settling back upon the bed. And I never saw Selliger play anywhere else. I wonder if I should tell Kazin. All too strange. These bracelets, identical crystals and his memory lapse. But Kazin puts us together. Too many puzzles for the first night in Jerusalem. . . .

Asher begins to drift into sleep gently, soothingly, as if Jira's hands were stroking him toward a deep indigo valley, sending him slowly toward a vast meadow, a magical forest filled with wondrous game.

Where Jira awaits him in a flowing golden gown, seated before a crystal chessboard. Lit by the final rays of the sun.

"Jira," he finds himself whispering. And is soon asleep.

13

G wyneth and Sefer are at each side of the bed.
Gad, propped up by pillows, is sipping his orange
juice slowly, gazing vaguely beyond the curtains swaying in the morning breeze. The Japanese yew tree which stands
before the window looks particularly fresh on this cool autumn
day; the sun is playing hide-and-seek through the mist, giving
the light a dismal dying quality, making Gad feel so much
sadder, so much worse.

Gwyneth, fresh-scented, lively and seductive, her hair soft
before the neck of a mint-green cashmere sweater, seems a
Botticellian allegory—the last vision Gad wishes to possess. He
is too weak. He is naked.

"What happened, Oliver?" asks Sefer politely.

Gad twirls the glass of juice with frustration.

"I told you. I became somewhat carried away."

Sefer nods and moves to the window, massaging his neck,
staring across the lawn toward the other Georgian apartments,
hating every one of them, their self-assured contentment, their
luxury, their ease. Oliver Gad certainly knows how to live well.
In a way, this is a plus for Sefer. After all, they'd never discussed
salary. Perfect mobility has Gad, perfect cover, perfect means.
Sefer turns from the window, smiling lightly at his protégé.
"Once more, please."

Gad looks at the sheets with a schoolboy's embarrassment.

"I shattered a light bulb. I bent a letter opener. I moved several volumes off the shelf. Then the place simply . . . fell apart."

"Simply?"

"For God's sake, Sefer," Gad protests, turning away from Gwyneth with frustration, "all of a sudden he was grabbing his throat . . . !"

But Sefer remains unperturbed. "Tell me what you saw? What image?"

Gad frowns, mumbling, "An ape."

It comes out quickly, automatically. He feels absurd.

"Mine's a nasty snake," says Gwyneth.

"Your *what?*" Gad grumbles.

"Your lower self," Sefer replies clearly.

"What the hell are you talking about, the both of you? An ape, a snake. . . ."

Gwyneth smiles. "Haven't you ever had a psychic attack?"

Gad scratches his jaw reflectively.

"Go ahead. . . ."

"You create a thought form of whatever it is you wish to appear: a dog, a leopard and so forth. You invest the form with energy, desire; you charge it with emotion. Then you remove the leash and let it go. The Ape just popped out of you, Gaddy." She smiles, with terrible charm, to Sefer. "The problem our Ollie has is that he could be a great magician, but he refuses to come to an understanding of lesser magic."

"That is?"

Gwyneth shrugs a bit too lazily. "Witchcraft."

"I didn't conjure anything," Gad spits.

Gwyneth continues to smile. "The Ape's part of your lower nature, your lower self. You never reached *beyond* yourself. . . ."

She pauses, letting Gad feel the effect of her words.

Gad stares stonily at Gwyneth, hating her as a wounded child hates the moral schoolmistress. "You said *killing* was only an option. That it wouldn't happen."

Gwyneth holds his gaze. Her eyes seem to pierce a thousand

years, to contain a million more. "It was. But now you've learned about your Ape, haven't you? You *did* project it."

"And your boa," Gad spits, almost bitchily.

"Mine stays in its cage."

"Has it always?"

She doesn't answer. Sefer interrupts the pair, ego-locked as they are, dangerously so. "Whatever happened, Mr. Gad, you were out of control. It must not happen again."

"Unless it's necessary?" Oliver adds ironically.

"You've that option, but if you ever take it, don't expect me to cover for you. I'll deny it most assuredly. Now then, what did you learn?"

They wait. Gad lets them wait. Then he reaches to the bed-stand and passes Sefer a piece of paper. "Here's your man. His name's Todi. He's in Rome. Evidently he gives V. K. the word, and the Dutchman sends money into an account in Liechtenstein. Called Yesod."

Gwyneth starts to laugh. "That's the Astral Plane in the Qabbalah."

Sefer nods, fingering the paper. *"Yesod . . .* that means Foundation in Hebrew."

"I wouldn't know." Gad shrugs.

"Very well. I'll trace this man. Shouldn't be so difficult. Meanwhile, have your rest, and we'll be in touch." Turning to Gwyneth: "Coming?"

Gwyneth looks at Gad worriedly, but he turns away.

"No," she says, "I'll take a taxi later."

"As you wish."

Neither Gad nor Gwyneth speaks, even as the door in the hall closes, even as they listen to the sound of Sefer's feet upon the gravel.

"That's why you're sick, you know. . . ."

Gad does not respond.

"You used up all that energy, sending out the Ape."

Gad turns away, staring at the yew tree, the misty sun seemingly caught in its branches.

"It's a wonder you made it back to London," she continues. "When it happened to me, the first time, I spent six weeks in hospital. I thought I was having a nervous breakdown."

"I want out," says Gad.

But Gwyneth shakes her head. "Never. Not to worry, Ollie. You also have a Higher Self, what the ancients call the Solar Angel. All part of the same process. Find your Prince, it'll be worth the effort. That's what it is, you know: The Warty Frog kissed by the Princess, and out comes the Prince. Lower Self illuminated by its higher complement. Those old tales are not off the mark. . . ."

"Stuff it, Gwyn," he snaps.

Gwyneth takes his hand in hers, toying with his palm. "I understand your fear, Ollie, really I do."

"Then let me be alone with it!"

Gwyneth is surprised, then hurt. She is out of the house in less than a minute.

Oliver Gad's fear has not been lessened by explanations given by Sefer and Gwyneth of his astral ape. Rather, he now knows he is a zookeeper in a fetid pit of slimy, subnatural creatures. A Guardian of Hell. The sobs come out of him, wretched, lung-searing and from a distance beyond the finite.

Oliver Gad, for all his sorrow, is beginning to question his evolutionary options.

Slowly he rises from the bed and crosses to the library, his body shaking still from the fever and the tears. He pulls a volume from the shelf, sniffling, and sets himself snugly in the armchair, shivering still.

And he begins to read:

"Once upon a time. . . ."

PART
TWO

Everything's in the mind. Everything's created and destroyed by the mind. It's the mind, it's not any devil's magick, that makes and breaks our mirrors and mirages.

—John Cowper Powys, *Maiden Castle*

1

It made the *News of the World:* BIZARRE DEATH OF A DUTCH-MAN—STRANGLED, BUT WITHOUT A MARK!

Sefer has read it twice, appreciating the science-fiction quality of the prose. It would put the Opposition on notice. It would be realistic enough to the Opposition: We've a chap in the field equal to your own; we've our strange superman as well and can counter tit for tat.

Sefer had pouched the coded query to Colonel Wharton, the military attaché of the British Embassy at Rome. In less than an hour the answer arrived at his office, and the decoding was begun:

Sig. Umberto Todi, Italian Director, International Refugee Committee, home v. Flaminia Vecchia 173, office v. Nazionale 146. Jewish. Interned in Yugoslavia 1942–43. Partisan 1943–45. Socialist. M., two sons: Egidio, doctor in Padua; Ettore, Slavic languages professor, Prague, Bologna.

Enough clues to write a book, thinks Sefer, leaving the office and crossing Hyde Park to a pay phone. He dials a private number, is connected at once to Mr. Carmel, the cultural attaché of the Israeli Embassy.

"Care to have a drink at the hotel?"

The bar at the Athenaeum Hotel off Curzon Street is empty, save for two loud, bearded Hollywood producers awaiting the arrival of the Star. They are discussing astrology.

Sefer and Carmel move to a corner. Each orders tea.

Eli Carmel is a tall, lean man with the face of Quixote. But there the resemblance ends, unless one still considers the existence of the State of Israel a quixotic fling in History's teeth. Carmel quite naturally did not, and was dedicating his life to making others aware of its reality. Sometimes, sad to say, his own government.

A brilliant tactician, as knowledgeable in diplomacy as in the theory and techniques of terrorism, Carmel had twice been dismissed for games above and beyond his office; seven West German corpses could attest to his skill, as well as the victims of that raid on a tiny East Norwegian village, site of a Palestinian network operating throughout northern Europe. Carmel was at times an embarrassment to the Israelis and yet a warning to the Palestinians and their libertarian supporters in the European extreme Left. But only three people in the world knew Carmel's true role. Sefer was one of them.

"Here's the man in Rome," Sefer begins, handing Carmel a slip of paper. "At the heart of emigration."

Carmel nods coolly. "And *your* man?"

"Why do you presume it's a man?"

Carmel allows himself a smile. One day he would learn the identity of Sefer's ward. In a matter of time.

"Went a bit crazy, evidently," Sefer says.

"Can you use this person again?"

"Of course."

"Here's our tea."

They drink in silence, Sefer doing the pouring. Carmel seems elsewhere, his mind running through the list of the members of the refugee program.

"So. I was right about the Dutchman." He sighs.

Sefer agrees. "He's a drop. Sends money to the Roman. Did it twice before, six weeks ago."

"That makes three," Carmel nods. "Well, should be simple

enough to find that bunch. Nice to know we've put the Sovs on notice."

"Give them a run, I should think."

Carmel smiles. "Sometimes it's hard to think of you as a Jew from the way you speak."

"Don't misread me."

"I never have. . . ."

Carmel rises with characteristic impatience. "Stay on top of your protégé. We may require further service."

"In how many days?"

"Give us a week. I want to know who went in."

"Can't you headlock the Roman?"

"Should be easy to muscle him," Carmel affirms. "But I don't want it tipped. If any more time bombs are coming through, I would like to know who it is that's sending them. Our Roman gets the word from Somewhere. And our Somewhere gets the word from Someone Mighty. The Dutchman was a snap. This Roman is a nuisance, but I don't want him dead. They might pull him out anyway, since he's the link." He pauses, fingering the silver teapot, running his hand along its edges. "Want my job?"

Sefer, surprised, finds himself smiling. "If I did, what else would you be good for?"

Carmel shrugs. "At the Sorbonne I delivered a paper on St. Anne and the Virgin, according to the stylists of Amiens. That's what I'd like to be doing. Taking photographs of Gothic sculpture. Not an ego in the place. All dead artists, all unknown. Why they ever called it the Dark Ages is beyond me. Well, thanks for the tea."

Sefer orders another tea and tries to sift through what Carmel has said:

Van Kessel to Todi to Somewhere to Someone. Todi's more important, obviously, but still at the practical bottom of the list. There has to be an intermediary, someone to dial the Dutchman and then to notify his own superior of the transfer.

Carmel obviously held the master plan, but needed to fit the actual players into it. It was Carmel who had brought Sefer the information about the Soviets' use of psychics. It was Carmel who had pointed him toward the Dutchman. What else did the man know?

Damn!

Sefer excuses himself to the waiter and dashes through the lobby of the Athenaeum. He stares down toward Hyde Park Corner, then up to Piccadilly, catching sight of Carmel's plaid cap in the crowd. Rushing toward the man, panting still, he calls, "I almost forgot: Check to see if these émigrés are wearing the same perfume or perhaps a talisman. Something of the like."

Without saying a word, Carmel nods and continues strolling in the direction of Piccadilly Circus.

Sefer curses himself and begins to move back to the hotel. His annoyance at his own forgetfulness is such that he formulates an immediate plan to deal with his charge's emotional state. He must bring him down. Connect him to the reality of the game if ever he is to be used again.

At the bar he places a telephone call.

"Mr. Gad?" he begins politely. "Thank you very much for your help, but I'm afraid our people find you laughable."

And puts the receiver down, breathing heavily still.

That should bring the little bugger down to earth, thinks Sefer. Feeling so much better.

Eli Carmel stands before the entrance to the Royal Academy of Art, wondering whether or not to return to the embassy. He needs time to think about his conversation with Sefer, to digest the material, to play with the options, then to act. The superficial pressures of embassy business do not concern him now.

He pays the entrance fee, to move through the corridors slowly, to build a Gothic church around the frenetically screaming works on the walls. Their egos shut him out immediately. He longs for one Poussin. All right, he thinks. Slowly, from the beginning:

All the phenomena I've studied—the busted apparatus on the Metro; the jamming of the radar; the Soviet broadcasting at the time of the Peking earthquake—all of it points to the group dynamic of psychics, the energy link between them. But what is the point of sending more time bombs into Israel? Do these people know each other and so link up? Are they conscious operatives in the field?

My task is threefold: to locate the émigrés; to find their source behind the Iron Curtain and destroy it; most important, to deflect the émigrés from their immediate goal, whatever it could be. Sending a psychic of my own to Amsterdam, and on such a low-level job, had been meant to let the Soviets realize their own game had been discovered and that our people are ready to play equally hard.

Carmel knew of Gad's raid even before the Englishman boarded the return flight from Schiphol to London. His contact in the Amsterdam Metropolitan Police had radioed on the frequency feeding directly to the embassy. The man in Holland had assessed the destruction, an excited observer. It had been a mess. An extraordinary mess. Nobody'd been seen entering the shop. Four and a half hours had gone by before anyone had even taken notice of the place. The feeling, he had to admit, was eerie and unsettling.

Carmel could console himself on one level: However potent the psychics seemed, still they were human and would slip up eventually.

Eli Carmel passes before the meat-and-carcass horror of a Francis Bacon. He is shocked, forgetting, for a moment, the meat-and-carcass of his own experience.

This is perhaps the worst century in recorded history, he thinks. And thus thinking, attempts to find a means to console himself.

He begins to wonder: *Why?*

2

Oliver Gad's physical and psychic collapse was followed inevitably by an emotional one seemingly greater than the others combined. This was natural enough, for his emotional rooms were well lived in and had provided him with well-worn comforts and familiarity of details. He was lazy, like most human beings, and depended on those comforts. Yet the psychic dungeon had blown a hole through the floorboards, and the drafts were keeping him sneezing and rheumy. Knowing of those treasures, moonstone and Rhinegold, was enough to make him take to bed.

And now that Sefer had called, telling him that the whole project was canceled, he had collapsed. The fact that he should have been thankful and that his life could have continued in the old patterns, in the same emotional house, proved to Gad how much he wanted to explore those unknown cellars and dungeons.

He had sensed possibility in himself. Yet he'd behaved like a teenager having sex for the first time. (Fifteen years of clammy brooding, and in three seconds it's over!) Even more infuriatingly, he had relied on Sefer and Gwyneth to point the way, to set the target. He hated relying on anyone and realized now in his emotional crash the full extent of this dependency.

But there was something else irritating him, something that neither Sefer nor Gwyneth had mentioned: The Power exists. From where does it originate?

In all respects, this was a dangerous question. For if he were to search for an answer, he would have to distance himself from the process, even while performing it. If it were at all possible, he would have to become "objective"—a condition he didn't believe was possible.

Sefer's response to the question would be existential. After all, Sefer was involved in an active psychic war. The phenomena exist, are being used against the West. Who cares where the Power comes from?

Gwyneth would speak of angels and fairies. Perhaps she'd be closer to the answer, the Power or Force translating itself into those simple terms for her. But still, she was, had to be, involved in the sideshow, deterred from or deliberately avoiding the main event.

There was a more selfish question, and Gad, like Job, felt he'd earned the right to ask it: *Why me?* Gwyneth might have been onto an answer when she'd told him the fairy tale, when he'd read "Once upon a time," but he could not believe he was a victim of supernatural forces, a puppet on someone's fourth-dimensional string. He'd never thought about the concept of free will before, living as he did in a society where private habits were not only accepted but publicly praised.

Where could he go to continue these exercises? What was the name of the shop Sefer had mentioned? Certainly he'd not encounter him there if the project had been aborted.

In the elevator taking him up to Boulter's office, Gad closes his eyes, sees an alleyway. Somewhere near St. Martin's Court. Fog, a yellow light illuminating the mist. Whit-something. He sees himself leaving St. Martin's Court, crossing to another alley. Sees himself speaking with a wiry, red-haired young man

81

with bulging green eyes. "Julian . . ." he whispers, "Cecil Court
. . . Whitken's."

But his psychic reverie is interrupted as the elevator door
opens and Boulter himself appears.

"Thank God," says the humpty-dump capitalist. "I thought
we'd lost you to the Dutch."

Gad smiles weakly, following Boulter into the office. Gad
senses, rather, knows, his intuition about dumping the gilts
and equities has proved correct. Otherwise, Boulter would not
have been waiting at the elevator, alerted to Gad's arrival by
the guard below. Instead, he would have remained indisposed,
in his office, for the day.

"What do you wish? Even though it's early, I thought we
might have a Pimm's."

"Tea, please," Gad replies, nodding to Hester, Boulter's
Glaswegian secretary, his favorite soccer-fan-in-arms. Hester,
he has always sensed, is the only one in the Consortium onto
him. He'd made love, once, with Hester, and only too well—
intuiting her pleasure zones, forcing her indirectly to intuit
his own. She'd never been with anyone like him.

As soon as Boulter has closed the office door, he shows Gad
to his own favorite Regency armchair.

"Cigar?"

"No, Sir Bill. Not now."

"Well, then, what've you discovered in Amsterdam?"

Gad smiles and pulls the prospectus out of his pocket.

"I do wish you'd use that briefcase, Mr. Gad."

"Don't need one, thanks. Koningen Elemental. Seems as if
they're on their last legs. Felson's needs an opening on the
Continent. I think we could arrange a merger easily enough."

Sir Bill frowns, nodding. His eyebrows meet merrily and
seem to lock in the center of his forehead.

"Precisely. When I broached the matter to Lord Bunting,
he appeared most interested. Do you wish to proceed, or should
I send Walters?"

Walters? Gad would have laughed at the idea one week ago.
But he had changed, was changing.

"Fine," he replies, surprising Boulter by his magnanimity.

"Now then," continues Boulter. "About these three companies: Copley, De La Ware and Magneto. We purchased shares, nine million pounds' worth, and set the Price Index spinning. They've jumped, each of them, three and a half pounds in the last day. We expect them to fall two, but we'll still be ahead by ninety-five percent. Do you suggest we sell them when they hit one hundred?"

Gad shakes his head. "Hold on, as I told you."

"May I ask you a question, Ollie? What in bleeding hell are radionics machines?"

Gad grins, shrugging.

"Surely, you must have an idea?"

"Not the slightest."

"But that's absurd. Research thinks you know something they don't know. Off the record, I feel you owe me an explanation."

"Why do you ask?"

"Because Copley, De La Ware and Magneto build such things. None of us wishes to appear ignorant to the tune of nine million pounds."

"If you wish, I'll find out."

"Do."

"Anything else?"

"No. Not for now."

"Then I'll be off."

And out of the chair, and out the building, and over to Piccadilly Circus and into a small alley lined with bookshops, with yellow lights illuminating the mist. Whitken's.

"Julian? Julian Webster?"

The man looks up, surprised.

"How did you know my name?"

Gad smiles, pleased with himself.

"You've four pounds sixty pence in your right-hand pocket," he begins nonchalantly. "An advertisement for some sort of meeting in your left."

Julian grins, slamming the table with his fist.

"Hooray, a genuine article! My address?"

Gad closes his eyes.

"Camden Town. . . . No, actually Primrose Hill."

A gay, thinks Gad. Lives with a Greek designer.

"Splendid!"

Gad places his hand on the bill spindle, closing his eyes again, whispering to himself, "Stay down this time," keeping the Ape in its cage, feeling the same tingling in his fingers, the queasiness in his gut. When he opens his eyes, the young man has turned white. For the spindle is bending downward, looking comically obscene.

"I say . . . ," Julian begins.

"No," Gad intervenes. "Please don't call the staff. I'm not a freak. I'd just like some explanations. . . ."

Julian stares at Gad appraisingly. Is he making a homosexual approach? But Gad smiles, shaking his head.

"No, Julian," he drawls. "I'm not like that."

Julian grins once again. "I *am,* and I'm bloody faithful."

Gad nods. "Stavros is a lucky man."

"Here, you *are* a sketch!"

They take tea around the corner, at a Lyons: stuffy, dense, as insipid as an old maid's smile. They lean toward one another conspiratorially.

"You see," Gad begins, "all this has been happening to me within the past month. Mind, it doesn't bother me, though it's quite awkward when I think about it. I feel as if I've X-ray eyes. . . ."

"But why did you come to me?"

Gad smiles. "I saw you. Saw the store. Knew that you understood these things."

Julian shakes his head. "I don't believe you. . . ."

"Please."

"But how did you know of our bookshop?"

"You've an accountant, an acquaintance of mine."

"Joseph Sefer?"

"Yes. He'd mentioned how odd the store seemed. Of course, I never told him about my . . . problem."

"Then you didn't see me at all?" snaps Julian, unconsciously hurt.

"Of course I did. Just as I knew where you lived, the contents of your pockets and the fact that your friend is Greek, and called Stavros, and that you've been three times to his family home on Siphnos. . . . His sister, Corinne—"

"All right"—the young man laughs—"that's quite enough. What do you want of me?"

"Tell me where this power comes from."

Julian sighs, then shrugs. "I can give you a historic summary, but it won't answer your question."

"Please," Gad urges.

"Very well," sighing again. "Were you a Jewish seer, in the line of Moses and Isaiah, then I'd say the power's—"

"No, no," Gad cuts him off. "It's not that."

"Tibetan?"

"Right now," says Gad. *"Here.* In England."

Julian begins to laugh at the man's impatience. "Any physicist would say your power is merely an as-yet-undiscovered natural law, an undefined extension of your sensory apparatus."

Gad shakes his head, waving away the remark. "What do *you* think it is?"

Julian begins to toy with the sugar bowl.

"Well, I can't quite accept the Christian definition, that your power is celestially inspired. The Tibetan conception of animism strikes me as more correct, in the sense that everything in movement possesses consciousness and that we can interact with and affect that consciousness. The Tibetan doctrine seems elegantly simple and thus possibly more correct. As an example, let's use the Burmese fire walkers. Suppose that I, as a child, see my father walking across a bed of coals without burning the soles of his feet. He tells me that his respect for the Fire Spirit protects him from the heat. Simple as that. As long as the Fire Spirit protects him from the heat, then I accept the existence of the Fire Spirit, and so I may also cross the coals and emerge unscathed. . . ."

Gad sighs. It isn't what he is after.

"There's more to it than that, Julian."

"Not much. Recognition of consciousness in all things may well protect me from the flame. I test myself. I am unscathed. Consciousness exists, as I always knew. Milarepa, the great Tibetan Master, controlled the clouds. Why? Because they were in movement and so had consciousness. He merely had to learn their language."

Oliver grins. "My friend Gwyneth would agree with Milarepa."

"Gwyneth?" asks the young man. "You don't mean Gwyneth Powys?"

"Yes," says Gad.

"My cousin."

Gad begins to laugh.

"Then that's the *second* person you mustn't speak with, about our conversation."

"If you wish . . . but how do you know Gwyneth?"

Gad looks at the table, coolly. "It's unimportant. About this Milarepa: If he could affect the clouds, where did that power come from?"

"From within himself. His uncle had thrown Milarepa's family off their own lands. Milarepa desired vengeance, studied with a black magician for seven years, then returned to cause havoc."

"So he believed in forces from other planes or levels of existence?"

"He didn't believe. He *knew*. To my mind, the old magical grimoires, the *Key of Solomon the King*, the *Book of Abra-Melin*, all the Cabbalistic reference works are filled with instructions which might explain the phenomena to you. There must be some truth to it, since the Church has gone about trying to suppress magic for over two thousand years."

"Have you. . . ."

"Performed magic?" Julian smiles. "I haven't the will for it, nor the desire. Most of my acquaintances are stuck in the glamour of it. Temples and wands, Crowley and the Golden

Dawn, that tripe. Mind you, I'm not doubting the effect of much of Crowley's work—just that his ego was insufferable, and again, he became stuck in the glamour. However, he was an extremely learned man. . . ."

"These magicians, do they believe in other forces?"

"Of course. The Qabbalah is something you might consider studying. Obviously you're in need of a road map. . . ."

"I daresay," Gad assents.

"It might appear rigid to you, but it's not. At the shop, I've several excellent texts."

"Recent?"

"Certainly. Magic hasn't vanished, you know. The Qabbalah's what you need—no use mucking about with tantric stuff; it'll just confuse you."

Julian stretches, looking about for the waitress.

"There's Knight, Butler, sensible fellows. Will Gray's work I find quite good. But remember, it's only a system. Once you know the rules, you can break them."

Gad nods. "I'm glad we've met, Julian. . . . I've felt so stupid about these things and rather alone."

"I'm sure it must be difficult. Where do you work?"

"In the City."

Suddenly Julian laughs and claps his hands, staring openly at Gad. "Hello! And here I was hoping you were Labour!"

"But I *am.*"

"Infiltrating, then. . . ." A crafty smile spreads across his face. He snaps his fingers. "Of course! You're Oliver Gad!"

Gad nods, almost shyly.

Julian whistles. "You *are* in trouble, luv. I know my cousin. 'Unimportant,' my arse." Julian grins conspiratorially.

Gad's features remain impassive. "Please don't mention our conversation."

"Wouldn't Gwyneth *love* to know! But how did you meet that old fart Sefer?"

Oliver looks away, stifling a fraudulent yawn which gives him equally fraudulent social distance. "I've dealt with his firm many times. He's one of their brightest accountants."

"Small world," says Julian, and refuses to let Gad pay the bill. If only for the pleasure of outreaching the Silver Fox.

At Whitken's, Oliver Gad buys William Gray's *A Self: Made by Magic,* the two volumes on the Qabbalah by Gareth Knight and Halévi's studies. Julian insists upon giving Gad a Tarot deck. "Quite special," he says. "Designed by our own Gwyn. Privately printed in Denmark."

Gad is surprised. "She never told me."

"Does she know of your abilities?"

"I think she's aware of them, though I've pooh-poohed the thing."

Julian cocks his head slightly. Gad knows he doesn't believe his reply.

"Her deck is different from the rest," Julian says. "Still, you may use it to follow the texts."

Gad thanks him effusively, suggesting a dinner at his club within the fortnight.

Julian shrugs, a bit too carelessly. "Remember," he begins. "What you're about to learn is a road map of psychic forces. Don't decide to go off on your own exploring. Well-lit, well-marked highways are what you're after."

Gad is about to thank him when he remembers his Boulter mission.

"By the way, Julian, what are radionics machines?"

"Mechanical dowsing."

"Excuse me?"

"It's a machine that tunes into the radiational pattern of any organ or emotion or even thought. The basic idea is that everything you possess contains a complete radiational picture of yourself; it could be in a piece of hair, a toenail, your handwriting or even an article of clothing. And from that force-field pattern you can analyze any physical condition or emotional state or mental picture, thought form, if you will. And if you are able to receive information from the pattern, you may also implant information into it. I don't know much about them. We've a few interesting books on the subject. Tansley's,

George de la Warr's. . . . From what I gather, it may well be the medicine of the future."

Direct hit! thinks Gad, and purchases Russell's *Report on Radionics* and Tansley's *Radionics and the Subtle Anatomy of Man.* All the books, all the data seem to serve as intellectual support for the experience of the past days.

Julian puts a hand to his sleeve.

"One other thing. A successful magician always has his feet on the ground. Most of the ones I know act as if they belonged to a secret and superior society. It's not worth it, Mr. Gad."

"Oliver," Gad corrects, irritated by Julian's unconscious deference.

"Be natural—if that's possible in this time and place."

Gad nods, walking into the tiny court.

He is beginning to feel human once again, with the kind of optimism that has taken batterings before and still rears its foolish head.

He'd discover what Sefer's game really meant, and he'd play it higher than anyone else.

Higher than even *I* can imagine, he thinks, accepting what he already felt to be but until now would never have openly admitted: *The existence of Higher forces.*

It was a flight that would wrest the moon from the hands of NASA and return it to its rightful worshipers: the poets.

3

The day after Joseph Selliger and Asher Berman had their initial discussions in the dormitory of Hebrew University, the Soviet government systematically begins to jam the World Service of the BBC and Radio Israel's international program: at noon, fifteen-, eighteen-, twenty-one- and twenty-four hundred hours. Each jamming lasts for nine minutes.

The radio waves are bounced, then scattered, interfering with the broadcasting of Radio Baghdad, the Voice of America, the Italian RAI and Radio Sweden. A complaint is issued by the respective governments.

But the jamming continues.

The day following Asher Berman's impotent discussions with Selliger about Prague, Mr. Michael Kazin meets with Hirsch, the conductor and director of the Radio Israel, to discuss a special refugee concert. First there would be a chorus of Yiddish melodies; a translation into Hebrew of the Soviet émigré poet Belinsky; two café songs of Asher Berman's; then, finally, Bartók's Third Piano Concerto, played by Joseph Selliger and the Israeli Symphony Orchestra.

It will be aired locally.

And broadcast over Radio Israel to northern Europe.

4

Sefer receives the call at two-thirty in the morning. A taxi is already on its way.

He throws water on his face, dresses quickly, then moves down the steps and into the damp London night. His lungs ache from the heavy pressure of the air.

Without a word, he enters the cab. The driver speeds off, accepting Sefer's silence.

He knows where to go.

Eli Carmel is waiting in the basement of the Israeli Embassy, off Palace Gardens in Knightsbridge. Sefer follows him through the garage entrance and into the dark, slumbering Georgian rooms.

"Over here," Carmel motions, ushering Sefer into a small office. Against the wall stands a motion-picture screen. Before it, a cool, mean-looking young man fiddling with a slide projector. Iraqi, thinks Sefer.

"Is this your office?" he inquires politely. Carmel points toward the room above.

"You've a view of the Serpentine," Sefer says. "Delightful."

Carmel shrugs. "Perhaps when your people begin to take your branch seriously, you too will have a view of the Serpentine."

"I rather think not," Sefer laughs. Carmel smiles.

"Continue to help me, my friend. Eventually, they must view you with favor. Even if at present the work appears to be a kind of embarrassment."

Sefer looks at the older man appraisingly. "And do your people view what can only be called psychic fascism with the same disfavor as mine?"

"Come now, Joseph; you know the old story. A flood of mythic proportions is forecast to occur in twenty-four hours. Panic everywhere. Except for a rabbi who informs his congregation, 'Smile; you have twenty-four hours to learn how to live underwater.' "

With that remark, once again Sefer feels the weight of M15, the whole Establishment on his shoulders. He'd been properly, humbly crushed. Save for a microflare of resentment which he'd displayed only once in his career but which had led to the formation of his one-man branch, the psychic limb. It was as if the shade of Cardinal Manning and the Oxford Movement were still haunting the citadels of power, condemning Mages and Sorcery.

He recalled his preliminary meeting with Carmel in that same Athenaeum Hotel bar. Before the contact, his Superior said that being a Jew would give Sefer a sort of edge with "that Israeli chap, the one who's always one-upping Arafat."

The bargain had been simple: Give us a man to help test this new psychic weapon, said the Israeli, and we'll give you all the data we possess.

Sefer, upon seeing the strength and resolve on Carmel's features, knew at once that the favor of information would have its price.

"Why can't your own boys do it?" Sefer had countered, and Carmel replied, "We don't want them to. Enough of our chaps are in the field as it is. Besides, though the Soviets and the Americans still use the Middle East as a playground for new weapons, sooner or later Europe will be the target. You might as well take advantage of the knowledge we've acquired."

A bad answer. The Sovs wouldn't suspect Blighty. That was the answer.

And yet the sprouting of the psychic limb had to be well orchestrated. More meetings were established between Sefer and Carmel, and occasional hints dropped to Sefer's Superior as to their content. Nothing specific, mind you. The thing takes a bit of stirring before it rises. Can't topple the old order overnight. The implication being that this new order, this psychic one, had to be presented as slight, interesting, a bit odd and basically unthreatening.

"Care for a joint meeting?" asked Sefer. "With my Superior? I do think it's time."

The information with which Carmel had provided him—spoonfeeding him gently, the care and feeding of babes born into a new era where mind energy rather than mind product would turn the cold war into a psychic one; where nuclear weapons would be but bowstrings by comparison, all the arguments supported by horrific data only the most dreamy could understand—hadn't Carmel done to Sefer what he himself eventually would do to Gad? Ease him into it? The enormity of it? The adventure?

Carmel attended the meeting, presented evidence, and when Sefer's Superior asked if he felt Carmel was certain about the Russian psychics, Sefer replied that Carmel most assuredly was.

"Still," reflected Superior, "I can't give you a man."

And the bargaining had begun.

"I require none," Sefer had replied, knowing that he was being asked to make one. To make a man.

"How do you expect me to authorize this new research? I've to go to the others, ask for funding. No, no, it just won't do." He said *do,* thought Sefer. Not *work.* He wanted the branch buried. Unknown to everybody, save Sefer, Carmel and him.

"Don't authorize the branch at all," said Sefer, which was what he'd been expected to say.

"But the financing?" sighed Superior, for how could he account for an invisible branch?

"Perhaps this is not for my ears," Carmel interjected. "But can we not transfer joint funds to the Anglo-Israeli Trade Commission?"

"The *what?*" snapped Superior, annoyed by Carmel's interruption of the dance. Let Carmel think Superior was just another British bureaucrat slouching toward his pension.

"A branch of the Chamber of Commerce, off Brook Street," informed Sefer.

"I know nothing of the branch at all," Superior replied. "I know less of the funding. Sefer, *do* look into it."

Carmel glanced worriedly to Sefer, but the latter already had risen and was nodding a goodbye to Superior deferentially.

"I don't understand you people," Carmel whispered forlornly.

"Nothing to understand," Sefer smiled. "We've just sprung a very secret limb."

Carmel stood in the hallway, astonished in spite of himself. "But how?"

"They order these matters differently in England," Sefer replied. "Oh, and before we begin, you're not to know the identity of the psychic I'm to train. We'll call that person Wand. Are we agreed?"

Carmel nodded. "Certainly," and immediately was determined to discover the name of that entity he felt entitled, after all, to consider his own godchild.

And so Sefer had begun to develop the psychic branch, his own weak, mewling babe alone in an uncharted forest, with only one tenacious Israeli as occasional guide. Sefer hated his indebtedness to the man but had to follow. Information was exchanged with Superior at parties, which was where Sefer had met Gwyneth and had learned of her occult powers. It was apparent she didn't give a damn for her husband, Edward, who was out of the country more often than he was in it. Their evenings, Sefer's and Gwyneth's, took on a more intimate nature. Sefer learned that she had been seeing Oliver Gad, Lombardy Street's Silver Fox, and the idea of a notorious, some would say slightly larcenous young stockbroker had seemed the perfect cover for a psychic spy. Gwyneth was certain Gad's business ability was due to more than education at the London School of Economics. Certainly his lovemaking had not been acquired from a manual.

It was intriguing to Sefer. Learning more about Oliver Gad, he realized the man was spiritually an anarchist. Everybody hated him at Boulter's, save Boulter and a few of the secretaries. And Sefer hadn't wanted to use Gwyneth herself yet, for she was still unaware of the branch. There had to be a way to get at Gad, to twist him, for he was the type who would never accept King and Country on his own.

A remark of Julian Webster's, as always, had supplied the answer: "A great magician is one who could dematerialize his own funds without the Inland Revenue Service ever getting wind of it."

But of course. Though Oliver Gad was not yet the budding magician, such a larcenous thought must never be far from his mind. Two calls to M15 operatives in Guatemala and Curaçao gave Sefer the lead. The Silver Fox did indeed bury treasure.

A knock on the coffer, and Gad was his.

"We've two problems," Carmel begins, "but one of them the Russians seem to be solving for us, so let's dispense with that first."

He hands Sefer a batch of papers.

"This is a jamming schedule. Our boys picked up the signal. It's not random this time. Quite systematic. Everything in multiples of three. The focus is on Radio Israel, the BBC and Voice of America. I'm convinced it's not so much a typical jamming as it is a piggyback. So the Russians are using our signal as well as the BBC's and the Americans' to ride on. The jamming began exactly twelve hours after the appearance of this announcement in the Israeli papers. Here."

He hands Sefer a newspaper. A column is circled in red. It reads: "Welcome to Israel: A program prepared by Soviet Refugees."

Sefer smiles. "You planted this?"

But Carmel shakes his head. "Didn't have to. If the Refugee Center is infiltrated, it wasn't necessary. Follow the refugees for a while, and something comes up to link them with their keepers. Here's the list of participants in the program. Among them, five arrivals in the past two months. Using the Russians' own magical arithmetic, let's assume that three people are all they need to effect their work. I've managed to isolate two of them—Asher Berman and Joseph Selliger. The third I don't know yet. It's not Belinsky; we've been over his background. It's someone in the chorus."

"Good work," whispers Sefer. "Pick up the pair, then substitute another program on the day of the broadcast."

Carmel holds up his hand. "Not good enough. I'd like to let the broadcast occur, to see what the Soviets have prepared."

Sefer frowns, but Carmel dismisses his concern. "Don't worry, Joseph. We're going to arrange for the VOA to 'minimize' its broadcasting. No way the Soviets can piggyback them."

"And the BBC?" asks Sefer politely. "If you don't mind, I'd rather not tip them off to the existence of our branch."

Carmel smiles mischievously. "Good. Then let's use *your* psych."

"Really? And how?"

"To knock out your transmitter."

"Nonsense."

But Carmel continues, imperturbably: "If we can get a thirty-second delay in the Israeli program, that will give Wand time enough to scramble, if not knock out, the BBC World Service. Meanwhile, whatever the émigré trio is programmed for will remain—shall we say?—a local phenomenon." He pauses happily, watching Sefer's eyes for the effect of his words. The blow is yet to come. "Unless, of course, we turn the broadcast against the Soviets."

Sefer looks away, frowning. He doesn't like the implication at all.

"Is it possible?"

Carmel nods. "By stepping up the local transmission while the Soviets are piggybacking *us,* we'll piggyback *them.* After all, with the BBC and the VOA paralyzed, the Sovs have only Radio Israel to rely on. Afterward we'll monitor the results in Russia to find out exactly where the damage is being done."

"You make it sound so simple."

"It is."

"I don't like it. You've too many assumptions."

"It's my job."

Sefer doesn't answer; he is playing for time.

"How can my psych knock out the BBC?"

"Telekinetically."

Carmel shrugs, continuing. "And so it goes," he says softly. "As you yourself have admitted, Joseph, you'll have to do it this way. M15 doesn't want the exposure."

Carmel is correct, thinks Sefer. The bastard.

"And if Wand is caught?" he snaps. "After all, you're putting the psych at the base of an extremely well-guarded transmitter."

"Don't be foolish. Your Wand must be in Rome."

Sefer looks up, surprised.

"Besides, Joseph," Carmel continues imperturbably, "I've done the homework you requested about talismans. All your charge needs is a crystal to wear and a crystal attached to the transmitter. Wand's thought waves will move from one crystal to the other."

So *that* is the unguent, thinks Sefer. The glue connecting Man to God; then he files the thought away, his features as still as a lake below a gathering storm.

"We've not done much telekinetic work."

Carmel smiles. "There's time. Your Wand doesn't have to go to Rome yet."

"Why must the psych be in Rome?"

"To force the names of two contacts out of our Italian friend

97

Signor Todi. He's going to need a show. Wand, from all reports, can give it to him."

"Decent of you. How much time do we have?"

"I'd like Wand in Italy the day of the broadcast. I'll have our people arrange to bring the Italian to our embassy."

Sefer nods. "That gives us. . . ."

"Three days to train. Flight to Rome. *Et voilà.*"

"And I give my psych away."

Carmel pauses, watching Sefer. "You give away nothing. False name, false passport. My word, Joseph. We'll take no photos."

"I'll keep up *my* side," says Sefer.

Carmel nods, smiling amusedly. "In other words, you'll take no responsibility for what happens during the program?"

"Of course not."

Carmel stares. "You think it's foolish?"

"I do."

"What makes you think I don't?"

"Then why are you doing it?"

"Because *they* are doing it."

Carmel rises from his chair and begins to pace the office. He turns, ruminatively, to Sefer. "The earthquake was a direct beam from Mongolia. They used psychics, this we know. In the '73 war, they used psychics as well. Now since their goal—whatever it is—depends upon the *combined broadcasting efforts* of the Americans, the British and the Israelis, I'm convinced everything that went before it, the earthquake, the melting, was but a five-finger exercise. The whole development is too clean, too linear. So now they are going to use our facilities, our beam. And to show you I'm not that much of a fool, Joseph, *here's* where the BBC, the VOA and Radio Israel will be broadcasting at the time of the refugee program."

He turns to the Iraqi, who nods and activates the projector. A map of the world appears on the screen.

"BBC: *northern Europe,* specifically Scandinavia and Holland. VOA: *the same.* Radio Israel: *the same.* What does this mean?"

Sefer pales. Carmel notes this, nods. "May I suggest a tidal wave? Storms to produce vast flooding? Cracks in the dikes? The crippling of the major ports of the world: Rotterdam, Hamburg, Lübeck, Amsterdam, Copenhagen, Stockholm? Think about it. Paralysis of the northern ports means paralysis of the Western economy. Plus the drowning of a million people in the bargain. That's my thesis." He pauses, staring at Sefer. "Three psychics, Joseph. That's all it takes. At any rate, if the thing works, we should be able to destroy their transmitter, go on record that we can play their game. Incidentally, about Amsterdam, the Sovs know something happened. Their military attaché was quizzing everybody about it at a dinner party. As subtle as a bear in a fish market. 'Tut, tut, horrible, what a mess, how could it possibly happen?' "

Sefer rises, directing his glance through the gold-corniced window and into the darkness. "I think you're taking a terrible chance, going ahead with that broadcast."

Carmel nods. "True. Up to you to lessen the odds of disaster. Wand could be of great service."

"Do your superiors know of these plans?" Sefer asks, almost wistfully.

Carmel sighs. "Are you questioning my capacity?"

Sefer shrugs. "Your intelligence."

"What would you do in my case?"

"Take the pair out of the broadcast. Locate the third psychic. Interrogate them. Learn where they've been, how they were programmed. . . ."

Carmel smiles and turns to the Iraqi for support. The latter shrugs. "Truly, sir: do you think we've that much time?"

Sefer says nothing. Wonders: *Why does Gad do everything in threes? And the Russians?*

"Very well," Sefer replies coldly. "What else is there to see?"

"Our pair: Berman and Selliger. Then various photographs of the Italian. And here. . . ." He snaps his fingers. The Iraqi hands him a tiny pouch.

"Crystals?"

Carmel nods. "Want to see the pictures?"

But Sefer shakes his head, knowing Carmel has revealed only the tip of the iceberg.

"Tell me the truth," he begins. Carmel is surprised. (So he *is* holding out, thinks Sefer.) "What are our chances?"

Carmel shrugs. "Let me put it to you this way, Joseph: if I hear of the slightest ripple in the North Sea, I promise you I will personally shoot Berman and Selliger, and in front of the entire Israeli Symphony. . . ."

He pauses, massaging his jaw.

"My God, man, I'm not that dumb. And yet, with their deaths, we will have lost everything. . . ."

Sefer knows this to be true. But he must be assured of other precautions, other contingency measures.

"I'm sorry, Eli—"

"We need them alive, yes, I know, but I'll have them shot if need be. As for the Roman, I don't give a *damn* about him. Let your Wand overkill, for all I care! Now, these crystals—"

Sefer smiles, recognizing Carmel's weariness. He sees it in himself and is more than sympathetic. "I understand. Before the war, the lover gave her soldier a lock of hair; the priest blessed the baby; the Mage charged an amulet. . . ."

"It connects," says Carmel. "A lock of hair, a crucifix, a Mogen David . . ." Then, almost a sigh. "My God, does it connect. . . ."

5

Gad has set the Tarot cards before him in a series of three, beginning with the Mage (1), the High Priestess (2), the Empress (3); then he began another series with the Emperor below the Mage (4), the High Priest (5) below the Priestess, and the Lovers (6) below the Empress, continuing thus until he had reached the twenty-first card, *the World*. But what of Zero, the Fool? Should it be placed at the beginning of its journey, before the World? Or at the journey's summit, above the Mage?

The other cards—the Spheres, Qlipoth, the Arrow and the Master Set—lie at his arm. The phone begins to ring. Gad picks it up, hears the familiar voice and drops the receiver on its cradle.

Mentally he begins to walk up the Tarot paths.

Then down again.

Gad has set the Spheres in their proper triangular series, Crown-Wisdom-Intelligence as the first; Compassion-Severity-Beauty as second; Victory-Glory-Foundation as third; the King-dom, or World, as the last.

He is mentally floating among the Spheres, lazily watching ideas grow into force, the forces themselves acquire form. Sens-

101

ing ideas develop into archetypal figures, Gad begins to watch mythologies appear, then civilizations, merging at last into the present world, sucked into the vortex of his finely growing perception.

As the phone rings once again, he shudders involuntarily. He lets it ring.

Gad sets the Tarot cards as paths linking the Spheres to each other. He begins to travel from its base, the World, and up to the next Sphere, the Foundation. The trip is dreamlike, the images lunar, silvery and dizzying. Each sphere has four levels, he thinks: Matter—Form—Archetype—Idea.

I can travel upward as if all the Spheres were Matter.

I can continue upward as if all the Spheres presented the Formation of civilizations on earth and in other galaxies.

I can move further and see everything as Archetypal, beyond historical man.

Finally, I can shoot beyond that dimension, to Higher Idea.

So it *is* a map, after all.

But where does the Fool belong? he wonders as the doorbell merrily sounds.

"Why, Mr. Sefer," he drawls, "you've come to the house of the Fool."

Sefer looks at the cards spread on the table and nods.

"Gwyneth's work," he says. "When did you last see her?"

"I didn't."

Sefer does not reply. There is an embarrassed pause, which Gad fills, gesturing at the cards. "This is excellent theory, you know; but how do you put it into practice?"

Sefer senses an opening and points to the window. "Out there, I should imagine."

"You're such a sod," Gad snaps. "If I can't put it into practice right here, in my breast, I'll never do it out there."

Then a strange thing happens.

Gad senses, rather knows, that he is watching the both of them, Gad and Sefer. It is as if he had left his body, suspended above and spying. He feels nauseated, fights to control the nausea. Sefer senses the dislocation.

"What is it, Oliver?"

"I'm not . . . not here. . . ."

Sefer nods coolly. "You're out-of-body."

"If that's what it's called. . . ."

"Can you move outside?"

The suggestion is enough.

"I'm beyond the yew tree. . . ."

"Gwyneth . . . ?"

"Right . . . she's in the bathtub, the ruddy bitch . . . here, she's looking up. . . ."

Gad suddenly feels a blackness, a spin, and lands heavily back into his body. He is sweating profusely.

"Want to puke. . . ."

"Close your eyes," says Sefer, quickly reaching for the telephone. "Breathe deeply and slowly," dialing all the while, waiting an inordinate length of time until the receiver is picked up by Gwyneth.

"Sefer here. Were you in the bathtub?" he whispers.

"Yes, I'm still wet. Let me get a towel. . . ."

Sefer looks at Gad and grins. The Silver Fox is turning green.

"Go over it again, Ollie," says Sefer, hearing Gwyneth put the phone down on a stand. "How did it happen?"

Gad shakes his head. His breathing is hard, tight. "I was looking at the Fool, thinking: If I can't put it into practice right here. . . . Then I was off. . . ."

Sefer nods, turning away as the receiver is picked up once again.

"Just a moment, Gwyn. . . ." To Gad. "Why did you return?"

"She made some sign at me. . . ."

Sefer nods.

"Gwyneth?" into the phone again. "Why did you make a sign in the bath?"

"I felt an entity," she snaps, her rigidity covering embarrassment.

Sefer laughs fully, richly. "That was no entity. That was our Gad. I'm afraid I'll need the both of you. May I pick you up? Say, in an hour?"

"Stuff it," Gad replies. "I'm not coming."

"You were out-of-body, man. And I must ask you to come because it is *most* urgent."

"I thought I was laughable."

"It was a slip. Please excuse me."

"It was intentional, you bearded bastard. And Intention is all, as the both of us know. . . ."

Sefer assents, politely. "It drove you to the Qabbalah, rather than to drink. A fortuitious sign. . . ."

Here we go again, thinks Gad. The old Master-Slave. Then it becomes obvious. "Did you know that Sefer means Book in Hebrew?" he asks.

Sefer nods. "I told you, weeks ago."

"That these Spheres are called *Sephiroth?*"

"Indeed."

"Then you *can* explain a great deal to me."

Sefer smiles. "That was my intention. You needed the slap, and you took it well."

"So it's back to Wales," Oliver Gad sighs.

"Bring your cards."

"Of course." Then it is Gad's turn to smile. "And don't think I won't have my revenge on you, Mr. Sefer. I owe you at least one."

"I will be prepared."

"Perhaps," Gad smiles. "But on which level?"

6

Asher Berman is meeting Mr. Kazin in the restaurant at Mishkenot Sha'anim. The inn, warm still from a thin but indolent sun, stands above the Old City like a fortress, its windows as shining cannons in the winter light; the cupolas of al-Aksa Mosque and the Dome of the Rock glitter like the spun glass of a fairy tale. Asher is silent, involved with the view. He'd gone once with Joseph into the Old City. They'd walked through the *suq,* visited the Wailing Wall, the Church of the Holy Sepulchre, but he'd felt nothing, had been too confused by the movement of tourists, the cries of vendors to make sense of the place. Besides, most of his days had been spent at the university, studying Hebrew.

But now, in the restaurant, the depth and extent of the Old City under winter light is beginning to make itself felt, to penetrate his bones with its liquid beauty. He finds himself crying. Five thousand years for that space, that spiritual whirlwind: Jew, Christian, Moslem, each had retained a piece of it, had carried it in his soul as a talisman. Asher is almost proud of the fact that he can state, "I understand nothing of Jerusalem. Only its beauty." Then he thinks: Is the battle for nothing less than possession of the beauty of Jerusalem?

Kazin rises, holding out his hand. With him is a middle-aged American in a tan shirt, tan slacks, tan shoes, nondescript tan features.

"Asher? Over here. This is Mr. Philip Weston, from New World Records."

Asher nods, shaking Weston's hand, then sits opposite the men, turning once again to the window.

"Welcome to Israel, Mr. Berman," says the Tan Man.

"Thanks, Mr. Weston. I'm certainly proud to be here."

Weston is shocked at how quickly Asher throws his own inflections back at him. Is he putting him on?

"Mr. Kazin tells me you're to give a concert at the end of the week," Weston smiles, scratching at his creeping gray sideburns. "I said I'd like to meet you. You know, we represent a lot of recording artists, and one of them is Celia Graves." Asher stares dumbly at Weston, who continues to nod encouragingly. "She calls herself the White Goddess."

"In Russia," Asher begins, "the goddess has been outlawed since 1918."

Weston laughs politely. "Well, Celia knows your poetry, Mr. Berman. We even had a translation of several of your songs made for her. Your 'World War Three, That's for Me' has been a hit in the States these past four months."

Asher is stunned. Immediately the comedy drops from his voice. He turns to Kazin. "What does this mean?"

Kazin shrugs. He doesn't like it. Any of it.

"I don't know."

"Don't worry, Mr. Berman," Weston laughs, laying a hand on his sleeve. "We put the money in a special account for you in Los Angeles. Whenever you come to the States, and I hope it's soon, you'll be free to use it."

Still, Asher is confused. "You recorded my songs? Without my permission?"

"How could they get your permission?" Kazin interjects with exasperation. "Don't be stupid."

Weston interrupts him quickly. "There's no copyright agreement between Russia and America, Mr. Berman. How many

American novelists have ever received a ruble from Russian sales?"

"So what does that make me in America?" asks Asher. "Ernest Hemingway?"

"Something of a pop hero, Mr. Berman," Weston replies, with arch seriousness. "Why I asked Mr. Kazin to meet you is because I'd like to have a contract with you, to record an album with you and Celia together. You performing your songs in Russian, Celia singing the translations. Perhaps the both of you doing a duet, it's completely open and up to you."

Asher shrugs, nonplussed. "Listen, Mr. Weston, I am just a *cafénik*. My friend Selliger, there's an artist!"

Weston turns curiously to the older man, who explains Selliger's background, his talents. Weston, unconcerned, listens politely.

"We're not really a classical company, Mr. Kazin. But I have friends at RCA and Deutsche Grammophon. I'd certainly be happy to do what I can for this fellow."

Suddenly Weston looks up and rises. "Well, finally, here she is. . . ."

A tall young woman is striding into the restaurant, wearing high leather boots of many multicolored patches, a white leather skirt, white turtleneck sweater, leather vest to match the boots. Her hair, long, white and full, hangs loose below her shoulders. Her eyes of gray-blue seem to swim rather than to perceive. When she grins, she appears slightly out of control. As she focuses upon Weston and the others, however, her gaze becomes clear, if not frighteningly direct.

"Celia?" calls Weston. "Mr. Kazin, and your idol. . . ."

But Celia is already upon Asher, hand outstretched, smiling with a frankness embarrassing to everyone.

"My *God*," she says. *"Finally!* I never even knew what you looked like." Asher is slightly ashamed. Is her warmth genuine? Fake? Genuine fake?

"And what do I look like?"

Celia stares long, then turns to Weston. "Kind of like Lenny

Bruce. Honestly, Phil, doesn't he remind you of Lenny?"

Weston smiles politely, thinking: How does Celia know Lenny? She had to be underage when he was around. Will wonders never cease!

"Listen, I think you're a genius, and I'm so happy to meet you." Pausing. *"Finally."*

"I have never heard your music," says Asher, "but I am sure you have excellent taste. . . ."

Celia laughs loudly, wildly. She is off-base and senses it. He doesn't know her, doesn't know what she means in America. Her praise alone is worth a platinum record. She prides herself on her directness, her honesty. She makes a living out of it.

"Phil's too polite, Mr. Berman," she begins, and Asher smiles wildly. She is the kind never to *mister* anyone, and they both feel it, they both know it. She pauses, waiting for him to say "Asher." He doesn't reply, however, eyes wide and deceptively innocent.

"What I'd really like is to go over your songs with you, the ones I haven't heard, and work on the lyrics in English. Then we could record them and after a few months go on a tour across the country."

"Asher Berman meets White Goddess?" he asks, with naïveté. "Should I not change my name to something more profound? New World Records presents White Goddess and her friend . . . Victor Shmeckle? I could follow you like a Chassid, with *payeas* and a *yarmulke,* my nose dribbling. . . ."

She laughs, can't stop laughing. Weston and Kazin are embarrassed by the heat of her laughter. But her laughter this time is genuine.

Sensing this, Asher begins to doubt the wisdom of his earlier feelings.

He continues: "We must appear onstage with a musical complex called *The Protocol of the Elders of Zion.* At the end we bring you onto the platform, tie you up and sacrifice you in our nefarious ritual!"

"Jesus, he's like Lenny, what is it?" she explodes, laughing through tears. "What are you on? *Speed?*"

Asher turns to Weston for understanding. "Do you take drugs?" the man interprets.

Asher turns politely to Celia. "Nobody has yet offered."

Weston waves a finger warningly at his gold mine. "Cool it, Ceel. Let's just get at least two albums out of the guy before you corrupt him."

Celia turns to Asher pensively. Her look of humor has dropped for an instant, enough time for Asher to perceive the craters of the moon. Or an altar, perhaps, with a woman beside it. A woman in white or of marble.

He shudders, yet the feeling, surprisingly, is pleasant.

"Do you wish to make this record in Israel?" Kazin begins, interrupting their heat. "We've excellent facilities—"

Weston looks down at the table, toying with his napkin. But Celia interrupts. "No way! My guys would be out of control by the time they flew over here from the Coast. It's bad enough just touring with them in the States."

"But Mr. Berman recently arrived in Israel . . ." Kazin begins.

"Hey, man, it's *my* album," Celia whines.

"Hey, men, it's *my* music," Asher mocks. "And if I am to understand this discussion, I am going to fly around the United States with the White Goddess and her band."

"Yeah," says Celia, "like I'm Stan Getz and you're João Gilberto. You're my discovery"—lowering her voice, leaning in, squeezing his thigh—" 'cause you *are,* you know. . . ."

"What is this White Goddess?" he asks embarrassedly.

"A name Celia suggested," Weston begins. "From the poet."

"*My* poet," she says, "Robert Graves. No relation."

Thank God for that, thinks Asher. She's claiming everyone else as her own.

"Does this mean I have to become an American citizen?"

"You're not Israeli yet," says Kazin. "Officially."

"Must I become an American citizen?"

Weston glances surreptitiously at Kazin. "No," he replies politely.

"Because I do not wish to be a citizen anywhere," Asher continues quite seriously.

"Far-out," Celia replies.

"Instead, I wish to become a representative of the planet Neptune!"

"Yay!" Celia cries, leaning across the table and kissing Asher, not for the effect it makes on the others, but for the ease and taste of his tongue. Unlike the others, Asher is not surprised. For his proclamation is meant to expose nothing less than the face of a goddess within marble.

7

The first target is a milk bottle set one hundred feet away upon a wall.

Oliver stares at it, and a piece of mortar slips noisily to the earth. Off the mark.

"Your force is an invisible hose, Oliver," says Sefer. "Think of it as a hose connecting you to the object. Send your thoughts through the—"

The bottle shatters at once.

Oliver sighs.

"A milk bottle's one thing," he begins, fearful of the Ape, refusing consciously to acknowledge it but knowing nevertheless that it is there.

Sefer, sensing his fear, touches his arm lightly and points to the roof. "The television antenna. Link the invisible hose to it. Nothing else."

Oliver nods, staring at the antenna on the roof of the house.

"The lower brace first," he says.

"I don't care which," Sefer adds.

"But I do," Gad replies, sighing deeply, then turning toward the antenna, lassoing the brace with his eyes, and feeling the heat rising from his spine, choking him as it reaches his throat, then spilling out through his eyes.

The brace turns red, begins to melt.

"By the way, Sefer," he says as the man continues to gaze in wonder at the antenna, "does the office pay you well?"

"Well enough," says Sefer, surprised.

"Good." With cool malice, Oliver holds out his right hand and points it at the tires of Sefer's automobile. Then he snaps his fingers. Four distinct pops. A wheeze as the tires deflate.

Sefer says nothing. Then, coldly: "How did you find the other side of the car?"

"I imagined it."

"In the future, *don't.*"

Gad glances up as Sefer points toward a milk van on the lane. The driver is out of the van, examining his own front tires.

"Follow instructions, please, Mr. Gad?"

Gad winces. "Dreadfully sorry."

In the cottage Gwyneth has set the crystal atop the candlestick. Gad, holding the other crystal before him and standing by the outside wall, is staring vaguely at it.

"Gwyneth's crystal makes the invisible connection. *It* is the end of the hose."

"But I don't know where it leads."

"Doesn't matter. Our decision."

"I'm not going to kill anybody, Sefer."

"Of course not. Now then, try to bend the object. . . ."

"But what *is* the object?"

"Doesn't matter. Just think of bending. Into the crystal."

Gad stares. Imagines an iron bar. Sends up the force from his spine. Imagines the bar bending.

From within the house, they hear Gwyneth calling, "Fine!"

"Now *burn* it," whispers Sefer.

The bending bar turns red, then dematerializes.

"Wonderful!" yells Gwyneth.

"Wait a minute." Gad calling, "Gwyneth?" Turning to Sefer: "Excuse me."

He runs to the house, all the while removing his wristwatch. Gwyneth is standing at the door.

"Hold this," he says, tossing her the watch. Then he trots back to Sefer.

Gad closes his eyes and slowly holds out his hand.

His body begins to tingle pleasurably. He is not the least bit surprised when Gwyneth gives a little shriek, and he himself feels the weight of the watch return, once again, in his palm.

"Dematerialization is so bloody obvious, and I'm no scientist," Gad begins. "To effect a bending, you shock the molecular structure of the object. To dematerialize the object, you shock it, then simply rearrange the structure."

Gwyneth smiles. "I have a lipstick on my dresser. . . ."

Gad nods, spots the lipstick in his mind's eye and snaps his fingers. Opens his palm. The lipstick nestles smoothly against the skin of his palm.

"My God," whispers Sefer.

"This is a sideshow," says Gad, wiggling his eyebrows. "Wait until the main event."

8

W hy do you have to do that stupid program?" asks Celia, removing her boots, then flinging them onto the floor. Asher looks about the hotel room, centuries removed from his university dungeon. Celia doesn't seem to give a damn about the place. Her clothes are strewn everywhere. Asher thinks: She is a capitalist pig with a Communist student's style. Then, remembering her lunarity: Perhaps she is neither. What do I know of these things?

"It's a promise I have made," he says.

"Listen, I have a place north of L.A. Weston doesn't even know about it. Why don't we split?"

"What is *split?*"

She is out of her vest, is stepping out of her skirt.

"Leave. There's a flight to London this evening. We could go from there right to L.A. . . ."

Asher shakes his head confusedly. "Why must we leave?"

" 'Cause I just wanted to meet you, to get to know you and to bring you back to the Coast."

"What makes you think, in fact, you know me?"

"You know what I mean," she murmurs. She is on the bed. She hasn't even bothered to remove her sweater. Asher wonders why.

He stands before her, dressed still.

"I cannot leave the country. I still have immigration papers."

She looks at him curiously. "Hey, don't sweat it." She reaches into the drawer, pulling out a dark blue passport. "Weston, Weston, he's my man—if he can't do it, no one can." She tosses Asher the passport, picking up the phone.

"Listen," she says, "I want two tickets out of here today, as direct as possible to Los Angeles. First class."

Asher is stunned. He stares at the passport, shaking his head. Then he takes the phone from Celia's hand, to replace it in the cradle. She looks up, surprised; eye-locked, she grabs him roughly by the arm, pulling him to her on the bed. His eyes, open still, are enveloped in white, the white of her sweater, her hair, her flesh. He feels himself falling in white. He hears himself laughing.

Then is surprised to receive the slap on his face, hard and stinging. And the way she takes his thighs, the roughness of her gesture. And before he begins to swim in a sea of sensation—what is it from?—he notes to himself that Celia Graves makes love with her eyes open and that her eyes, like a serpent's, possess no depths.

He watches her. He shakes his head slowly, as if in trance.

It is less an act of masculine penetration than of feminine envelopment.

> And on I go,
> Away, I see
> A way. . . .

The words are whispered by herself to herself, and alone, repeated densely; he understands nothing, clinging to her now, and when he comes, it is with a pain that seems to spasm upward from his gut. She whispers something in his ear, stroking his hair, singing.

"What?" he starts to say, but she shakes her head, holding him still.

And then he remembers the melody, he remembers what she is singing.

For it is his own melody, translated from a lonely cry to something mystical, occult and beckoning.

9

They are seated by the fire at the Heady Ram, above the Western Sea of Wales. Sefer, himself unmoved by the lush and dewy surroundings, is twirling a glass of bitters in his hand. Gwyneth and Gad, together again, are scarcely listening.

"Now piggyback," continues the bearded man, but Gad interrupts: "Once more."

Sefer sighs, puts down the glass and waves away the waitress.

"There are two distinct types of jamming. One is called scattering, where you shatter the radio waves, and what remains is static noise; the other is called piggyback, where you sit atop the other signal until both merge, the first fading, the second coming in, then the first returning, the second fading. Try to imagine the radio waves as two coiled snakes, the stronger of the two controlling the fading."

"By increasing the power of the signal?" asks Gad.

"Correct. But slowly; otherwise, it will become a scatter situation; piggyback is a delicate sort of jamming, while scattering's the norm."

Gad calls back the waitress, ordering a gin-and-bitters.

"And what am I to do?"

Sefer glances at the waitress, remaining silent until she has

116

gone. Then he explains everything, omitting no details: the broadcast which will produce the tidal wave; the knocking out of the BBC tower; Gad's interview in Rome, still troublesome to Sefer, for will Carmel learn of Gad's true identity? Sefer continues, uninterrupted, and when he has finished, Gad emits a long, low whistle. Even Gwyneth is silent.

"And all this in the next three days?"

"I admit we haven't much time. . . ."

Gad follows the waitress into the kitchen with his eyes. And then, surprising himself, he is *in* the kitchen.

"I'm sorry, sir," she begins pleasantly, "but we allow no one here."

Gad nods, smiling.

The waitress blushes for the liking of his smile, then turns and leaves the kitchen, crossing back to the table. Gad is seated there, once again, whistling. The waitress pales, dropping the drinks with a clatter, staring wildly back toward the kitchen door. Gwyneth and Sefer watch her, surprised.

"But, sir, how did you . . . how did you get here before me?" Her voice is trembling.

Gad does not answer. Instead, he turns to Sefer. "I don't think there'll be any need for me to go to Rome after all."

Sefer does not understand.

Gwyneth, staring at Gad still, turns to the waitress. "What is the matter?"

"When this gentleman followed me into the kitchen," she whispers, shaking visibly, "I told him. . . ." She cannot continue.

Sefer stares at Gad with an expression the Fox finds most enjoyable.

"Would you go to the car, fetch my gloves?" he asks. At first Sefer is confused, then rises to leave the inn and move down the gravel path to the car.

Gad is standing there, arms folded against his chest, legs crossed, leaning against the rear door and grinning like the Cheshire Cat.

Sefer is stopped dead cold.

117

"But can you speak?" he summons.

Too late.

For Gad has already disappeared.

On the road back to London:

"The method, Oliver?"

Gad stretches languidly, turning to Sefer. "I have the *idea*. I imagine myself *there*. I project myself with enough force, and off I go." He shrugs. "You suggested it, man."

"But you didn't speak. . . ."

"I was afraid to. What was I like in the restaurant?"

"You seemed to be dozing," Gwyneth replies.

"I was concentrating. Don't you think it's more important for me to be physically present in Israel? I could make one phone call to that Roman, project myself over the line and if anything happens bring myself back. The timetable," Gad continues, "should be: Go to Israel. Make the call to Rome. Work with the crystal to muck up the BBC transmitter. Then go to the broadcast and defuse the psychics."

"Our colleague wants them alive," says Sefer stiffly.

"That shouldn't be difficult."

"Our colleague also wants to blow up the Soviet transmitter, using the psychics' own power."

Gad frowns. "Well, he can't have both, can he? Will your contact meet me in Israel?"

"Naturally not. Leave Israel to the Israelis, Gad. We need you here."

Gad turns to the woman driving the car. "But if I took Gwyneth. Between the two of us. . . ."

"I can't come," she says, with a kind of finality that surprises the men.

"And why not?"

"Suppose something goes wrong with the broadcast and the sea actually threatens the coast? Someone has to calm it. . . ."

Gad begins to laugh. *"King Canute?* Is that who you think you are?"

"Don't be ridiculous."

Gad is shaking his head. "Canute tried to stop the sea. That, I presume, is Gwyneth's plan. She's the one who's being ridiculous."

"Moron," she drawls. "I don't intend to do it alone."

"What do you plan to do, then?" asks Gad sarcastically. "Call in the Royal bleeding Navy?"

"I've friends. . . ."

"Living or dead?" Gad smirks.

"Living, you idiot!"

"What are you both about?" Sefer interjects, thoroughly confused by the exchange.

Gad snorts, "Can't you see, Sefer? She's a *witch!* She wants to call on other witches and make contact with the Elementals."

Sefer says nothing, settling further into the seat of the car then sighing, "I am asking you to go to Rome, Mr. Gad. Spoonbend, toss books, do whatever it is you do. Shake the fellow up a bit. The rest is to be left to the Israelis."

"Bugger the Israelis."

Gad hears applause and turns around. Beside Sefer, vague in the rear of the auto, sits a warm, intelligent woman with long black hair and deep blue eyes. She is wearing a dress that reminds Gad of the Medici court. She claps her hands, smiling warmly at the Fox.

"Bravo, Sefer," he whispers. "Your Mireille is a piece!"

Mireille blows Gad a kiss and dissolves.

Gad turns to Gwyneth, looking for approval, but she is still frowning. He shrugs, nonplussed. "Bother. Let Gwyneth do whatever she wants."

"Very well," Sefer replies. "Though it will be difficult justifying your presence in Israel to Carmel . . . if I must justify it at all. . . ."

"Well, *she* won't go," whines Gad, staring at Gwyneth. "Will she?"

Gwyneth shakes her head.

"If I go anywhere, it will be to a place north of here. . . ."

"Can I guess?" asks Gad.

Gwyneth turns to him, smiling slightly.

Oliver looks into her eyes and feels the depths of the North Sea, swimming to a place in his mind where the sea gains its strength, where volcanoes bubble beneath the ocean floor and sulfur fumes spume mightily.

"Iceland," he whispers. "The seat of the Gods of the Northern Lands."

The image begins to shimmer, to wave in psychic heat. *"Das Rheingold?"* he asks.

"Fool," She laughs. "That came later."

"But Iceland was correct."

He knows he is right, and so does Gwyneth. But she acknowledges nothing.

Suddenly Gad is frowning. Something is wrong with her plan. He cannot define it. Not yet.

"Very well, then," says Sefer. "As for Gwyneth, she may do whatever she wishes."

"I'd rather she were in Israel with me," says Gad hopefully. "As my generator."

Gwyneth shivers involuntarily. "Doesn't matter. You're beyond that stage. Besides, I'd like to work with my friends again. . . ." She looks at Sefer in the rearview mirror. Excellent. He isn't listening. "I've your permission, Sefer?"

"Of course, of course," Sefer mutters, playing with Gad's plan, wondering how to plant the young man in Israel before Carmel learns of it. It *would* give him the edge. In case Carmel failed to shoot the psychics. Gad the Stopgap. Carmel would be furious, of course. He needn't know till after it was over.

"We should all be leaving tonight then," says Gwyneth, watching the frost form from her breath on the auto window.

"If you must," Sefer replies.

Perhaps he should tell Carmel, have him keep an eye on Gad. It would be a nasty affair, either way. Sourly he realizes it is neither Carmel nor he giving the orders.

Everything is in Gad's hands.

The Servant, he reflects idly, has become the Master.

Better not to tell Carmel. Let him believe Gad's on the plane to Rome. Let Gad do whatever he wants. In Israel, Sefer has

120

only one contact, one person reporting directly to him: Ilse Doyle. He'd put her on to Gad, arrange for her to meet him at the airport. Keep Gad locked until the broadcast. Then get him inside the building somehow. Afterward, out of the country.

"You're making things quite difficult for me," Sefer says to Gad, moving quietly into his plan.

"Two months ago," Oliver begins, "I was most happy in my ignorance. Wasn't I, Gwyn? Wasn't I happy?"

"You were amusing," Gwyneth replies. "But you weren't much else."

He is surprised and says nothing.

"Two months ago," she continues.

Her eyes gleaming.

Gad sits in the car, staring at the yew tree. The moon seems to be poised in its branches.

"I'll pick you up in the morning," says Sefer. "We'll drive to Heathrow together."

But Gad isn't listening.

"Gwyneth," he begins, taking her hand. "Give me something of yours. That ring. Something to connect."

But Gwyneth shakes her head. "This is *my* work, Ollie."

Sighing, Gad turns away. And in that sigh, Gwyneth's scarf dematerializes from her purse and lands in Gad's coat pocket. He stuffs it down even further. "Well, then," he drawls, "if all goes well, shall we try once again at the Brace of Pheasants? *Sans* Sefer and his dwarfs?"

Gwyneth smiles slightly, refusing to look at Gad. He reaches into the rear of the car, picking up his small leather valise.

"See you then?" he calls. "Say hello to the dolphins."

He waits until the car has driven away. Then he flags a taxi at the corner and gives the driver Julian Webster's address.

10

Sefer stands at the first pay phone, clasping the change he'd received from the pub. Gwyneth holds out her hand, and he passes her the coins, watching with some annoyance as she feeds the pieces carefully into the machine.

"Lisa, darling, how are you! . . . Yes, this is Gwyneth; I'm afraid I need your help."

Sensing Sefer listening, she slams the door of the pay phone.

The next call is made from Heathrow itself. It takes ten minutes for the operator to locate the woman of São Paulo.

"Astrud? Gwyneth here. . . ! Astrud, I need to see you. . . ."

Sefer waits for Gwyneth at the Icelandic Airlines desk, feeling exhausted, hoping she will simply disappear. There has been little time to contemplate, to assess the plan carefully. Gwyneth is impulsive, but at least she will be out of harm's way, somewhere in Iceland. Why Iceland? he thinks. Is she serious about this witching business? Keeping the sea safe from storm? Gad's materializations had been easier to accept than *this* rubbish.

Gwyneth turns gaily from the counter.

"I think this is going to be fun," she says. "You'll keep an eye on Ollie, won't you?"

"At all times," Sefer replies. "I'll even give orders to slap his face whenever he seems to go into a trance."

"Good. You won't be hearing from me until my return. But I'll need expenses."

"Your trip is not authorized. . . ."

"Not simply for *me*, darling. I've a friend flying out of Brazil tonight. Another coming in from Copenhagen . . . and I do like to live well. . . ."

Sefer sighs. "This one from Brazil, how is she flying?"

"Not only first class, Sef, but on the Concorde to Paris. Then from Paris to Reykjavik. But she *must*, darling, to be in time. Isn't that wonderful? She'll actually arrive before my Danish friend. . . ! Come on, Seffypoo, don't be a pig."

Sefer permits himself the luxury of an oink, watching her trot toward her gate without even bothering to wave.

11

The phone call comes to Kazin in the middle of the night.

"Levin, is this you?"

"I'm afraid not," Kazin replies. "You must have the wrong number."

"You are sure?"

"Absolutely certain."

"Very well. Sorry to have disturbed you."

Kazin smiles to himself before he turns out the light. Certainty has a wonderful effect on the psyche. The plan operating on schedule.

"Who was it?" asks his wife.

"Wrong number," he replies.

"Again?"

"Don't worry."

"Asking for Levin?"

"Yes."

He turns away from his wife, feeling her eyes staring at him in the darkness. "The third time in a week," she says. "Shouldn't you report it?"

He yawns loudly, grappling with the covers, pulling them over his head. "Tomorrow."

Certainty gives him the edge.

In less than a minute he is snoring.

124

12

"Oliver?"

The young man pulls the silken robe more tightly around his waist, then opens the door.

"Sorry to bother you, Julian."

"No bother at all. Come in, come in."

Oliver hears a scraping movement upstairs.

"I'm disturbing something."

"Family matters. . . ."

Oliver smiles embarrassedly but nevertheless enters the apartment. "I hope your friend doesn't think I'm. . . ."

Julian wiggles his eyebrows, leering. "A new lover? Let him think the worst. He deserves it. What may I offer you?"

"Nothing really. I've come from a trip. . . ."

"So I see," Julian replies, staring at Oliver's valise.

"May I sit down?"

Julian points toward a Récamier couch. Two enormous avo-cado plants stand guard at its feet. Oliver enters the sitting room, admiring the makeshift brick bookshelves, the hundreds of titles staring at him challengingly. Julian pulls a bentwood rocker to the base of the couch. Gad doesn't know whether to lie down or sit up. Instead, he chooses to recline.

"I assume you're upset, Oliver, or you would have called."

"Not upset, Julian. Worried."

"About what?"

125

"Gwyneth."

Julian looks away coolly. "Which aspect?"

Gad smiles. "The *witch* aspect."

"Oh, dear. I'm afraid you found her out."

"Matter of time."

"Quite. But what has she told you?"

"Not a great deal, frankly. Still, enough to cause concern."

Julian, glancing up the stairwell, sighs. "I'd rather not concern myself with that aspect of Gwyneth, if you don't mind . . . and it is rather late. . . ."

Oliver frowns, then closes his eyes, projecting himself into the bedroom. A dark young man is seated before a mirror, staring at his gums. After a moment, Gad returns.

"Your friend isn't upset by my visit," Gad replies. "He's merely concerned with his teeth. . . ."

Julian stares, surprised, then laughs.

Gad closes his eyes again. "He's gone to his bed and is smoking."

"What are you doing, Ollie? Projecting your double?"

Gad nods.

"Really?"

Once again Gad closes his eyes, seeing himself at the foot of the fellow's bed. He waves politely, disappears. . . .

Julian hears a scream, then a rush of footsteps down the stairwell. The dark man pauses as he spots Gad, then draws himself up coldly.

"Oh. . . . I . . . swore. . . . Excuse me. . . ." He turns to move stiffly up the stairwell.

Julian watches him leave, pursing his lips appreciatively.

"Very good, Mr. Gad. Now if you would project yourself home. . . ."

"Julian, I'm worried about Gwyneth. I'm afraid if you don't tell me, I will have to make life a bit more upsetting. . . ."

The leaves of the avocado plants are bending, as if a stiff northern breeze had entered the flat. Julian pales, shivering. "I thought we were friends."

"We are, and I want us to continue to be friends. Why won't you help me?"

Julian rises and reaches for a packet of cigarettes on the bookshelf, then pauses, lighting filter end first; then tosses the cigarette angrily to the floor.

"Here," says Gad quietly, and offers him one of his own.

"Ta. . . ."

Julian leans forward as Gad lights the cigarette.

"I really find your blackmail approach disgusting."

"Look, Julian, I don't have time. . . ."

"All right," he hisses petulantly. "What has she done?"

"It's what she might do."

Julian turns away, gazing vaguely at the bookshelves. After a moment he says, "If I tell you, promise not to go running to the police."

Gad nods.

Julian stares at him hard and long. Then he shrugs, plunging in. "Gwyneth is a murderess."

"There was a woman named Leila Kent, a dreadful person. Very attractive, but very evil. There wasn't a move she made that wasn't willful and calculating. And she was extremely intelligent. Gwyneth was only sixteen at the time, and Leila recognized her psychic gifts. Leila was a vampire and drained Gwyneth of her strengths, using her energies for her own ends."

"What were they?"

"The usual ends of one on the Left-handed Path: domination. She collected quite a little group about her. A sort of occult school. She gave the impression she was spiritually minded, and when the group level had been raised, she began to drain it. Gwyneth isn't stupid. She sensed the energy drain. The second time she felt it, she tried to leave the group. But Leila had begun to attack her psychically. Finally, Gwyneth began to turn the energy against Miss Kent. Before the entire assembly, poor old Leila choked on an apple and died. There was quite a scandal."

"Why?"

"She appeared to have been choked to death, though all the people swore she'd merely swallowed improperly."

"How did you know Gwyneth was the one who did it?"

"Because I was there. I caught her eye. Triumph is unmistakable, is it not? Leila remained on the Astral Plane, and Gwyneth ended up in a sanitarium for nearly six weeks."

Gad is frowning, his mind crisscrossed with extravagant ideas. To calm himself he asks, "What became of the group?"

"It disbanded. Several members stayed on, praying for Gwyneth. . . ."

Gad shakes his head, worriedly. "You called Leila Kent a vampire. Surely you don't mean—"

"Holes in the neck, that sort of thing? Of course not. It's a much less dramatic phenomenon: A vampire sucks a person's energy field to feed its own. Every normal family has at least one vampire, does it not? *Mine* certainly does. And these fat little gurus running rampant in the West, half of them are vampires."

Gad gestures, impatiently. "Did the authorities perform an autopsy on Leila Kent?"

"Certainly," says Julian. "They found the apple blocking her windpipe."

Gad pauses. Gwyneth's hidden ape. Rather, her snake. No wonder she'd been so self-righteous upon his return from Amsterdam. She'd seen the monster as well. She'd known it intimately.

"What exactly did the group do?"

"Meditations on the Spirit World. Dialogues with Elementals. . . ."

"Such as?"

"Spirits of the air, earth, fire, water. Forms of creation that materialize by the force of our calling. All those silly grimoires talk of it."

Gad shakes his head. "What were you doing in the group?"

Julian smiles bitterly. "Finding myself, Ollie, finding myself. After that experience, I'd found enough of myself to want out. Sometimes I regret it, but not really. 'If God wanted us to fly,' that sort of thing. I'm Roman Catholic now. Does that explain much to you?"

"Not quite. This Leila . . . is she still on the Astral Plane?"

"Good question. I never asked. Hopefully she's moved on. I doubt if she's incarnate."

"Could she still give Gwyneth trouble?"

"Not if Gwyneth's careful. If she's given up the witch business, everything should be fine." He pauses, watching Gad coolly. "Has she?"

"Has she what?"

"Given up the witch business?"

Gad shrugs, but with enough concern to cause Julian to feel he does not really know.

"And if she hasn't?" asks Gad.

"Then any force that Leila uses could come in from the Astral Plane and cause havoc. Worse, Leila herself might enter through a human channel, someone unstable or stupidly psychic. Not many psychics are spiritual, Ollie, let's not forget."

"Do you have a photograph of this woman?"

"A ceremonial portrait somewhere, surely."

"May I have it?"

Julian nods and crosses to the bookshelf. He brings down a box of photographs and begins to rummage through them. After a moment he smiles. "Here. Group photo of Leila with the Outward Bound. There's Gwyneth."

Instantly recognizable. Bright-eyed, with that saucy nose, coppery hair rich and long, eyes sensual even then.

"And here's Leila Kent."

Gad stares. "She's not much older. . . ."

"Don't be silly. She was over forty. Just the costume."

"Attractive."

"Of course."

"And these others?"

"Our group. *Those* girls were the ones who stayed to pray for Gwyneth. . . ."

Gad stares at a dark-eyed, wizard-cheeked young woman with thick black hair. Beside her, a hand upon Gwyneth's shoulder, a young girl as blond as the other is dark. Almost an albino.

"Who are they?" whispers Gad, immediately attracted.

"Astrud and Lisaveta . . . I used to call them Macumba Mama

129

and Wotan's Plaything. Quite interestingly, Lisaveta later became a physician. Actually not so interesting, since she was a natural healer. As for Astrud, I don't know what happened to her. She was a dancer for a time. . . ."

"May I take this photo?"

Julian frowns. "You're not going to confront Gwyneth with it, are you?"

"Of course not. I give you my word. And please, Julian, forgive me for that ploy. But you could be saving Gwyn's life."

Julian closes his eyes, waving a finger warningly to Gad. "I don't want to know a thing, thank you. I'm sorry, Oliver, but I'm convinced, even after all these years, our Gwyn's been marked for death."

Gad snorts. "And who isn't?"

Julian chuckles, his voice becoming airy. "You get back what you give out, ducks. And if I know Leila Kent, six weeks in a sanitarium is hardly the price to pay for choking on an apple."

Gad in his apartment, sitting in the bathtub, letting the warmth of the water play upon his senses. So Gwyneth *is* a witches' witch, he thinks with some amusement. She must have known all along what I'd been doing, what I was capable of doing.

Certain things she'd said—"My Company has other plans," references to a mission of a different sort—all those remarks in some way must have referred to the death of Leila Kent, to her group, whatever it meant. Old witch Gwyn, so alone now—yes, he loves her, though secretly he knows he mustn't interfere, for Gwyneth's battle is on a different plane, a different level, with a vocabulary and a weapons system he can't begin to understand.

Gad knows now, more, is convinced, his own gifts can be explained. The "double" is amusing enough, and his ability to dematerialize objects. But these have become for him parts of speech, *tools* rather than vision. The psychic's wonder bag of tricks finally is nothing but tricks, if wondrous it is at all. However, as an aspect of a larger picture, the power behind the tricks is beginning to give him a clue to his own greater, higher identity.

He had admitted fully to the existence of Higher Forces or Powers within and beyond himself. The human mind—if its energy were not being used as a weapon of destruction—could also draw upon its energy to create and to sustain life, linking up with those more potent, more evolved forces. How?

By evoking them. By resonating them within himself.

His mind, he knows, no longer resides in a tiny portion of his brain, but vibrates within and without his own body. His consciousness is everywhere. He is in a state of perpetual high.

Simply put, he knows that Matter *matters*.

Indeed—he thinks in his warm-water musings—this struggle's for something more, something beyond the noisy little spy games that keep the bleeding governments in business.

Gad rises from the bathtub, drying himself quickly, snatching at the robe draped across the heater. He crosses to his valise and pulls out the pack of Tarot cards.

It is there, the answer, in the position of the first card, the Magus:

Right hand raised heavenward, left hand downward. The Magus is Idea. The right hand is reaching for the force to realize the Idea. The left hand is pointed downward to use the force to create the form to give the Idea tangible, material shape.

Idea uses force and form to become Idea Realized.

But there is something else.

Pointing to the sky, pointing to the earth—a phrase he'd read in one of the books and which he had begun to sense as an operating principle:

AS ABOVE, SO BELOW

Idea has its realization in Nature. Nature is Idea Realized. Therefore, what happens on the planet, on the material level, must have its counterpart in the realm of pure Idea. Of course! That's what the four levels mean: Supernal—Archetypal—Formative—Material.

It was as if man's development had occurred in four psychic

131

stages: first, as Idea; then as Idea taking on the coloration of racial consciousness; then fixing itself, drawn down yet farther toward biological time; finally emerging as historical matter. As matter which is the product of Idea, given mental force and biological form.

Gad thinking, with childish delight: *Man is at root a Cosmic Idea.*

Darwin's Origin of Species is merely a half-truth since Darwin considers the biological origin as the essence of man. And all these behavioral theorists, Skinner, Ardrey and the like, these soulless statisticians, refuse to recognize or do not comprehend the Idea of Man *first as Idea.* They see man as a meat machine, a product of his own material instincts. They deny him the slightest degree of intuition, inspiration, yes, divinity. The emphasis upon the material has blinded them to the existence of the Idea. Mechanistic science, mechanistic behavioral studies or political systems deny the presence of Idea.

Why? *Because Idea not yet realized, not yet given form cannot be quantified.* To a mechanic, therefore, it doesn't exist.

And our desire to know, to understand, to become more than what we are is but an inspired recognition of our own origins in Idea. As above, so below. . . .

Gad takes another card blindly from the pack: the Fool.

He grins at himself in the mirror. Here I am, he thinks, about to perform stunts which two months ago I'd never dreamed existed. And alas, though I should be marveling at myself, I am content merely to shrug. What do I want? What am I after?

And then he knows, as always he has known.

I want to discover whose Idea I am.

13

Selliger glances up from the bed and sets aside the musical score of the Bartók piano piece, marking the measure he has been studying. Though he knows the work by heart, he must be sure of the other voices. The conductor could lose his way or one of the sections, leaving Joseph himself to set the pace. At last night's rehearsal, Hirsch, the conductor, had been surprised when Joseph had interrupted his own playing to say, "There's no slurring called for in this measure; why are the celli slurring the line?" Hirsch had expected a certain nervousness from his guest performer, from *all* his guest performers—he hadn't expected to be challenged by a young academic.

Worst of all, Selliger had been correct.

"Where were you?" asks the pianist of the bleary-eyed café-child Asher Berman. "We waited nearly an hour for you at rehearsal."

Asher shrugs, plopping onto his own bed, closing his eyes and putting his hand to his temple, massaging it slowly in rough, tight circles.

"I've been *shtupping* my brains for both of us, if the truth be known."

"You look terrible," says Joseph.

"I could no more sing today than I could tackle that damned language. Did you tell them I was sick?"

Selliger sits up in the bed, staring concernedly at his friend. "Are you?"

Asher shrugs. "I don't know . . . and that's the truth. Some people want me to go to America to make recordings. Evidently I am well loved in America. All the time I have been singing at the coffeehouses, they have been copying my songs and selling them."

Selliger grins. "Excellent!"

"What is excellent? To become a millionaire?"

Selliger raises himself on his elbows, leaning animatedly toward his friend. "I'm talking of the possibility of recording your work and having it heard. That's wonderful!"

Asher shrugs. "Wonderful or not, I'd just like to get it over with."

"What over with? What are you talking about?"

"That silly broadcast. These pressures. America sounds ridiculous, but perhaps it's the place for me. Maybe I should go to America before I become too attached to Israel. . . ."

And he thinks to himself: Fine point. If things don't go well in America, I can always return to Israel, the Prodigal Son. And Celia Graves seems stupidly promising.

"What time must we be at the radio station tomorrow?" he yawns.

"The broadcast is at nine o'clock."

Asher nods, closing his eyes.

He has promised to meet Weston and Celia later that evening, to discuss the technicalities his temporary American passport—if it weren't false—might raise. Perhaps in his sleep there would be an answer, a sign of sorts. There is still time to decide.

"Shall I wake you for dinner?" asks Selliger.

"No. Go without me."

Selliger shrugs, disappointed. "Very well."

And picks up the Bartók once again, and the pencil.

14

Sefer is slouching in the rear of the car, deep in the folds of his topcoat, more tired than ever he could remember. "Her name is Ilse Doyle. You're to stay with her. Make the call to Rome from her apartment. Under *no* circumstances leave the apartment until she tells you. Here are the photos of the two fellows you're to watch. And here. . . ."

He hands Gad a yellow envelope.

"Another 'fellow'?" asks Gad dryly.

Sefer catches the irony but is too tired to play with it.

"Unfortunately this man will be on the same flight with you. His name is Eli Carmel. Top Israeli Security officer. Though he doesn't know you, he knows of you. Please stay out of his way. He doesn't want you in Israel, and if he finds out you're there, it will be difficult. . . ."

"For you?"

"For both of us," whispers Sefer.

"Why?"

But Sefer doesn't answer. Gad has sensed the complicity between the two agents and stares at Sefer good-humoredly. "You've no support here, do you, old man?"

"Don't be absurd."

"What's my role in this? Will I be paid in English or Israeli pounds?"

Sefer turns away. "If you wish, upon your return, I will explain the arrangement between our respective governments."

"Stuff it," snorts Gad. "I'm up to my neck and prefer to go no higher."

"Then keep out of the man's way, Oliver. Do you have the crystal?"

"Of course. See you, then."

Gad leaves the car, tossing the crystal high into the air, then dematerializing it into his pocket. Expecting applause, he turns. But Sefer has driven away.

15

Celia and Weston are halfway through their dinner in the restaurant of the King David Hotel when Asher appears, bleary and unshaved.

"You're late," says Celia.

"Aren't you feeling well?" asks Weston solicitously.

"Metaphysically?" Asher begins. "Spiritually? In which sense?" Asher takes the menu from the waiter, stares at it, orders soup, changes his mind, orders soup again, then decides he isn't hungry at all. "A cup of tea," he replies, turning glumly to Weston. "Physically, I am feeling wretched. Spiritually, I am confused." Asher smiles at Celia, then makes a vulgar gesture, as if he were picking something intimate from between his teeth.

Weston catches the gesture, raising his eyebrows. "Celia was telling me you're . . . thinking of coming out to the Coast."

"The Coast?"

"To Los Angeles."

Asher sighs. "I was considering it, but as each minute passes, I consider it less and less. In ten minutes, I would not be surprised if I were to become senile."

Weston glances at Celia, who appears to be drowning in her glum and distant, bitchy mood.

"I don't understand," he says, frowning.

"I ask myself," Asher continues, "if this woman is as manic as I—which she is—is it because she possesses genuine artistry? Or is it perhaps because she believes her gift is the result of white powder, stuffed into sinuses."

Celia throws her napkin atop the salad, pushes back her chair and quickly leaves the table. Weston watches her go, then starts to rise. Thinking better of it—the contract, after all, has not yet been signed, the deal has not yet been made—he pulls his chair close to Asher's. "Celia's a great talent," he begins, "but very temperamental. She had a breakdown a year ago. Can we be straight with each other, Ash? Coming to Israel was her idea. And getting you that temporary passport. . . ." He lowers his voice, moving closer to Asher. "She wouldn't leave L.A. without the passport—you don't *know* what our Legal Department went through. She loves you, Ash. She loves your work. I don't think it's right to be so harsh on her."

Asher nods, thoughtfully. "Mr. Weston, I have been in Israel less than a week. I am not looking for excuses or sympathy, but I cannot feel sorry for someone as obviously successful as she; perhaps if I were as rich, I would be as self-indulgent. She is spoiled. Why don't you slap her face? Or spank her?"

Weston says nothing.

"When you finish your tea—"

"I am finished with my tea."

"I'd like you to come up to my room. I have a tape of her latest song, and yours. I'd like you to hear it. Give her a chance."

Asher shrugs, following the man out of the restaurant. Feeling thoroughly self-righteous, and a bastard.

Celia's recording—sung in a tough, wailing and yet oddly otherworldly voice—is about a trial in Salem, Massachusetts: "The Song of the Child-Witch." The refrain, "When my love cries out/I want you/Then my tears return/To haunt you," makes Asher feel embarrassed. Not so much by the simplicity of the idea as by the sincere urgency of her cry.

His own song on the other side of the recording—"World War Three, That's For Me"—has been filled with extraordinary sound effects, of bombs dropping, children screaming. It is grotesque. In performance, Asher had mimicked the bombs, had ended the song with a spotlight tight on his soundless, shrieking face. There was no need for Celia's overproduced effects. But perhaps he was wrong—he didn't know America yet. Her intention had been correct, and she *did* understand the irony of the song. He loved the banjo duet played against a background of air-raid sirens and crowd noise.

"When must we go to Los Angeles?"

"It's up to you," Weston replies.

Asher stares thoughtfully at the cassette. "Does Kazin know of the passport?"

Weston shakes his head. "No, and we'd sort of like it to stay that way, at least for a while."

Asher is confused, self-interest conflicting with the obligations he feels toward Kazin, Selliger and his uncle Kolya, whom he'd seen only once since his arrival in Israel.

"How did you know I was coming to Israel?" he asks, perplexed.

Weston smiles, crossing to his desk and handing Asher a batch of papers. "Don't you read the trades?"

"What is 'trades'?"

"*Variety, Billboard, Cashbox.* . . . Entertainment papers."

Asher stares dumbly at the texts, then looks at Weston, shaking his head. Weston squeezes his shoulder playfully. "We're a company, Asher. We make it our business to follow the careers of our artists. And like it or not, so far you're one of our artists. Look." He points to a chart. A song has been circled in red ink. "That's yours, man. Number two for thirteen weeks. This week, Number one. Celia believes in you, Asher, even more than she believes in herself—if such things are possible."

Asher is feeling like a fool.

"Very well," he says. "I will speak to her."

"Go," Weston urges. "Do."

In the towel-strewn hotel room, with the drawers and closets in a state of shameless disarray, with her wardrobe, books and magazines tossed in all directions, covering all existing space, Celia Graves is starting to pack.

"Well?" she begins, not even bothering to look up at the embarrassed Asher. "Coming?"

16

Gad likes Ilse Doyle immediately; her deep black eyes, offset by wrinkles from the extremes of history, are compassionate and lightly ironic. He imagines her to be in her late fifties, early sixties. Later he will discover she is seventy-three.

"You've come," she says simply, and leads him to the waiting car. Though he is tired from his journey, Oliver's senses immediately lift in the fresh, invigorating sunlight of the Holy Land.

Ilse does the driving. In her steady commentary on places she feels would interest him, Gad hears the accents of the displaced Londoner; passing Ramla, Ilse points out the prison; cutting around a burned-out Jordanian tank, she recounts the battles fought, drawing from the modern story its historical counterpart. But Gad is more intent on tracing her accent.

"Stepney?" he inquires, and she turns to him, smiling.

"Golder's Green," she says.

"From Sefer's speech, I'd say he's pure Golder's," he adds.

Ilse watches him appraisingly. "Wrong. He was born in Calcutta."

Gad grins. "Same thing?"

Suddenly Ilse pulls the car to the side of the road. Gad is

surprised and looks about him, expecting to see a historical site. Instead, he finds Ilse staring at him as if he were a Martian, a wry smile playing upon her lips.

"Tell me something," she begins. "Why are you here?"

"Long story," he replies, sensing exactly where she is leading. "However, if you think I've a Jewish problem—"

"The Jewish problem will cease to exist only when there are no more Jews," Ilse Doyle answers.

"I meant, anti-Semitic."

Ilse smiles politely, but her eyes are cold. "I would have said antihumanity. Before we go into Jerusalem, I would like you to see Yad Vashem."

Gad shrugs. He has the time. He is not to make the call to Rome until five o'clock.

"What you wish," he replies.

Ilse shakes her head. "No. Not what I wish. What you need. . . ."

And she begins to head the car toward a large and rolling forest.

"I hadn't expected so many trees," Gad says almost to himself.

"Nobody does."

"And does Providence enter into your scheme of things?"

Ilse shrugs. "This forest wasn't planted by Providence. While you are here, what are you to do?"

Gad smiles. "I will attempt to drive a man crazy, to blow up a tower, to stop a radio broadcast. . . ."

"Why not?" Ilse nods. "You've got twenty-four hours. And you're so very young."

She gestures toward a slim and attractive building in front of them. Yad Vashem.

It is not so much the immediate horror of the individual displays—the children's shoes, the enlarged photographs of the Warsaw Ghetto, the copies of *Der Stürmer* or even the scenes of the camps themselves. Gad has seen them before, as he has seen other horrors of war and of desolation. Rather, it is the accumulation of evidence, the extraordinary *numbers* and their necessary counterpart, the ponderous, gray bureaucracy that kept the trains running on their way to the camps; that manufactured the gas; that paid the wages of the men who ran the tractors for the corpses and who bought the petrol for the tractors to move the corpses to the graves. It was the tedium, spelling acceptance of horror and of outrage that stunned him most.

Gad finds himself choking with impotence and disgust. Not until he has arrived at the end of the display, where the numbers of victims are listed on a black map—so many Jews in Czechoslovakia before the war, so few remaining and so forth—that the nausea overcomes him.

He feels his way to the door.

Trees stand in his line of vision. And then Ilse, leaning against the car. For a moment she says nothing. Then: "Every tree is an act of thanks to those countries and individuals that helped the Jews. Now you can see why Israel has meaning for us."

"Why did you bring me here?" Gad asks quietly.

"Because whatever you do, you should remember *why* you've been sent."

"To help Israel?" he whispers, and senses in that word more than geographical commitment: a *longing.* A knowledge of home. "No," he replies. "To help myself. How strange."

It is in Jerusalem, in the vortex of the Old City, that his senses begin to jar him, to make him feel faint. The odors, intensified by the thin, steady sun, and the images: a glint of solar reflection on the Dome of the Rock; the harsh and pungent smell of incense from a procession leading to the Church of the Holy Sepulchre; the Chassidim like dark swans at the Wailing Wall. Moslems, Christians, Jews, each has a place here; the Jew has given birth through Rachel's handmaiden to the Moslem; through Joseph and Mary and the line of Prophets

143

to the Christ. Offshoots of the same Western tribe, yet limbs threatening to destroy each other and thus to destroy themselves.

That the United Nations condemned Zionism as a racist belief showed the same hideous lack of imagination that had produced the death camps, Gad *knows* now. It was a resolution which smacked of the banality of the charnel house. Israel, he realizes, is not a political issue, to be settled on battlefields or in diplomatic councils.

For who can settle what had always been a mystical union?

"Why hasn't Sefer told me about Jerusalem?" he asks later, in Ilse's flat in the Jewish Quarter of the Old City.

Ilse pours him another glass of wine.

"Who can tell anyone anything? You have to see for yourself. Jerusalem's a city; we have our whores and our crime. The sad fact is that every Christian and every Moslem is a Jew. When this is pointed out, people become irritable. I hope I'm not offending you, but whatever happens here will affect humanity."

Gad nods. In a strange way he senses she is right. He finds himself agreeing with her.

"I'm glad," continues Ilse, "I like you. You're the friend of someone I consider a very good friend. . . ."

"How did you meet Sefer?"

But Ilse shakes her head and points to the telephone. Almost magically, it begins to ring.

"Your call," she says. "To Rome."

17

Signor Todi has been ushered through the gates of the Israeli Embassy on Via Mercati, inspected by the guards while another gate opened; then he is accompanied to a small, pleasant office overlooking a semitropical garden. Beyond the garden itself stands a high wall. The Roman *poliziotti* are stationed in a jeep on the other side. Below the window, two plainclothesmen are patting a German shepherd. Since Rome has become the principal center of Southern European operations for the Black September Movement, the embassy has been transformed into a fortress.

"Signor Guglielmo, *shalom, shalom.*"

Todi looks up, surprised. Here is Ben-gal, the cultural attaché. Odd, since it had been the Ambassador himself who had asked for the appointment. Todi was flattered. Now he feels disappointed.

"I'm sorry," says Ben-gal, "but unfortunately, as you can see, the Ambassador has been detained. May I get you something to drink?"

Todi shakes his head. "Then to whom do I owe this meeting?" he asks uneasily.

"We need your help. But are you sure you won't have something to drink? A tea or something?"

Todi, feeling like a condemned man, shakes his head once again.

"Very well."

Ben-gal flicks the switch on the intercom. "Send in Bronsky and Tefelev. And has the call come in?" Ben-gal turns from the intercom, surprised to see Todi still standing.

"Please, please sit down. What's the matter? Aren't you feeling well?"

"The usual *mal di fegato*. . . ." Todi smiles nervously, wiping his brow with the palm of his hand. "What may I help you with?"

Ben-gal looks at Todi reflectively, then seems to become lost in his own thoughts. The door suddenly opens. Bronsky and Tefelev appear, nearly identical in stature, moving with the feline assuredness of killers. Todi senses this and turns to Ben-gal, who stares back coldly. Ben-gal feels sorry for the man. But he'd feel sorry for lots of men.

Bronsky hands him an envelope. Ben-gal opens it and pulls some photos from its interior. He nods, tossing them to Todi. "These are clippings from a newspaper. . . ."

Todi takes the photographs, the papers. He shakes his head. "What is this language?"

"Dutch," Ben-gal replies. Todi frowns. His hands are trembling. "As you can see, it is a bookstore. A total disaster, is it not? Oh, and here is the picture of the owner of the store. He was murdered. His name is Van Kessel."

Todi feels his face drain of blood. Why is he so outwardly frightened? Why can't he hide his fear?

The intercom buzzes.

Ben-gal flicks the button, says, "Keep him on the line" before the secretary has a chance to speak. Ben-gal turns back to the Roman. "We know he sent you money, deposited in an account in Liechtenstein. Named Yesod. You would ask him for Ficino, Bruno. . . ."

Ben-gal's voice never changes. Todi finds this amazing.

"Take a look at his face, Signor Todi. His windpipe has been crushed."

Todi shakes his head puzzledly, glancing up at the attaché. "Why would he send me money . . . ?" but his voice trails off. He turns helplessly to Tefelev, to Bronsky.

"We're not sure yet," says Ben-gal pleasantly. "But here—" He takes the telephone, handing it to Todi. The latter is stunned and shakes his head nervously.

"What?"

"It's Van Kessel's murderer. On the line. . . . ."

Todi holds the phone dumbly and puts the receiver to his ear.

"Todi?" he hears, almost a whisper. "Listen, you bastard, I want you to watch the wall, look straight ahead. . . ."

Todi, trembling, looks up, beyond Ben-gal. Slowly an image begins to form, a young man with gray hair and clear blue eyes. Todi's mouth drops open.

"That's me, Todi. Now watch this. . . ."

Tefelev and Bronsky have drawn their guns and are pointing at the figure. Todi turns to them and screams as the guns disappear from their hands, dematerializing into the ether.

"Todi?" he hears. "Todi, are you there?"

Ben-gal grabs the phone, shoving Todi back into the chair, bringing the piece up hard against the Roman's ear. "Listen to him, you scum!"

Todi is grasping at his heart, sweating profusely.

"Who sends you the names of the special émigrés?"

"I don't. . . ."

The man materializes again, handing the agents their guns. He starts to disappear, but not before he moves like a smiling phantom one inch before Todi. Tefelev and Bronsky are staring stupidly at their weapons. White, shaken.

"Asher Berman, Joseph Selliger, we know about them," continues the voice on the other end. *"But who is the third person?"*

"Zilpah," gasps Todi. "Zilpah Wallinchek."

"Any others?"

"One in Canada. I forget. . . ."

"Who tells you where to send them?"

Todi gulps. His eyes begin to bulge out of their sockets. He begins to clutch at his tie.

"Waldheim . . ." he rasps. "In Vienna."

"Who gives *him* orders?"

Todi is grappling with the chair, trying to steady himself, to keep himself erect.

"In *Israel?* Who's your contact?"

"Kazin . . . they're met by Kazin. Michael—"

Todi tumbles off the chair, holding his chest, eyes and knees drawn upward. Ben-gal stares at Todi as if he were a piece of dung; then he takes the receiver.

"Thank you," he says. "That's enough. . . ."

But the line, like Todi himself, is already dead.

Gad hands the phone to Ilse and closes his eyes wearily. His eardrums are throbbing. His lungs ache mercilessly. He feels like a fish out of water.

Gad takes a piece of paper, writes "Wallinchek—Kazin—Waldheim," then folds it, placing it in his pocket.

"Here," says Ilse, and passes him a cup of vegetable soup.

"A hard day's night," Oliver Gad sighs, sipping the soup gratefully. "Mind if I use the bed for an hour?"

Ilse smiles warmly.

"Ilse Doyle"—he grins—"I wish I were older."

"Be careful," she warns. "In the end you *will* be."

18

Gwyneth stands at the pier, watching the black waves toss and curl against the warpy gray sidings. Northern clouds, dirty and low, move ominously toward her from the east. The jagged pinnacle of Mount Hekla is soon lost from sight.

Gwyneth pushes her hair into the collar of the white windbreaker she'd purchased at Hafnarfjörđur, southwest of the airport itself, and gazes solemnly at the sea, heart center calm, mind empty, Gwyneth waiting until the magical event moves into frame like an old familiar friend. She turns toward the sky. The clouds smell of rain, frozen beyond the idea of snow, of moisture trapped in an icebound purgatory. Lightning forks through the clouds, and the waves are illuminated as in a nightmare's flash. It begins to rain.

Gwyneth hears the putt-putt of the fisherman's boat and turns. Lisaveta is standing at the stern, waving. In the growing dark, with her fair white skin and milk-white hair wrapped in her white mac, she resembles a Norse Princess. Astrud sits beside a gray-haired fisherman, talking animatedly, a dark vision almost comically out of place. Gwyneth smiles to herself.

And so they are together again, united in a circle of invisible force and form. For a moment Gwyneth remembers their faces, fading in and out of the sanitarium room, how they'd never left her side. And when she'd seen the snake, the grin of him, the stench, when she'd felt the dull, lethargic weight of Leila Kent pressing upon her chest, Astrud and Lisaveta had moved at once to clear her aura, to stand guard as psychic knights.

When she had been released, they had taken her to Lisaveta's cottage on the island of Hven, there to recuperate. On Hven the obvious paradigm of psychic attack (if someone rushes you, with a knife, move away; if someone lets loose an astral knife, move your astral self) had hit home with overwhelming force. On the island of Hven, she had chosen to rid herself of her occult knowledge, to close the channel connecting her with the world of the Elementals and the Forces on the Astral Plane. Lisaveta and Astrud stood as witnesses to her final ceremony. And the door connecting her with the death of Leila Kent seemed, finally, to be closed.

Yet Gwyneth's return to the world of the arcane had come about gradually, on a picnic with her gentleman friend Mr. Sefer. He had quoted a work of Blake's, she'd forgotten which, wherein the poet had spoken of grasses used in healing, of Nature's pharmacopoeia. Gwyneth had mentioned certain healing properties of clematis. Sefer was intrigued and drew her out further.

One night he had asked her to explain the Tarot cards, for he'd brought with him the Ryder deck, the old one used by the Golden Dawn. Gwyneth pooh-poohed it, showing him her own set, the one she'd designed for the final ceremony on the island of Hven, the one containing the forces, the essences, ideas and forms with which she had intimate connection. Sefer noticed immediately that Gwyneth had stripped her own Tarot figures of their cabbalist-hermetic symbols. Everything was clean, comprehensible and thus all the more evocative.

That same evening Gwyneth began to travel out-of-body on the Astral Plane. Gwyneth visited old friends.

"He says he'd better hurry," Lisaveta begins. "He thinks there'll be a storm." She holds out her hand to help Gwyneth

150

onto the boat. "He's given us the name of an old woman who rents rooms." Gwyneth nods and sits beside Lisaveta, putting an arm about her shoulder. Lisaveta smiles. Then they both turn and stare through the scud of cloud and sea mist and in the direction of Surtsey.

The island was a product of the mating of the oceans with the primal matter of the planet's core. It had begun as a slow eruption of gases that could be seen from Iceland itself. Then, as the gases gathered force, the island began to form, a new addition to the planet, created of boiling air, tumultuous fire, viscous, burning water and, when the substantial caldron had subsided, solid earth.

It was called Surtsey.

Its birth was the pride of sylphs, ondines, salamanders and gnomes. To a physicist, these are fairy-tale words for building blocks of matter. To a chemist, they may be reduced to a combination of molecules. To a working magician or witch, however, they are natural forces instilled through an act of intense concentration into workable form and thus made visible to the operator's consciousness.

Surtsey, as a preening child of the planet, had not yet been left to fend for itself. The island, connected still to the soul tissue of Mother Earth, was teeming with Elementals. Its youth and position in the North Sea is therefore vital to Gwyneth and to her friends, for ondines, sylphs, salamanders and gnomes could be conjured up by the magical art and asked to perform certain deeds, then to be discharged, with the knowledge of their sworn obligation. Or so Gwyneth hopes.

Rather than dampen her spirits, the black clouds covering the lulled, tense waters only give her strength. Her companions, settled into the boat, cheer her even more. She loves them, the sloe-eyed Brazilian Astrud, whose eyes seemed to reflect emerald forces and forest dreams made tangible; the stately Lisaveta, Scandia-souled, Astrud's opposite. They'd remained in contact, though none had ever mentioned the death

151

of Leila Kent. They had moved on, all of them, yet Gwyneth's recent out-of-body travels had kept their magical mood connection alive.

And now it was as if they had become girls again, sharing in that comfortable Georgian house off Regent's Park.

The boatman is pointing toward a low and smoky outcrop of black soil seemingly floating before them.

"Surtsey," he says, and Astrud begins to clap her hands delightedly.

19

Eli Carmel slams down the telephone, cursing.

Well and good, he'd the names of the major contacts, the Viennese Waldheim and that bloody traitor Kazin. But that wasn't the point. *Sefer* was the point, Sefer's sending that damned freak to Israel against his orders. He'd probably been on the plane with him as well. Wand had put on quite a show in Rome: appearing, disappearing, removing the guns from Ben-gal's bloodhounds, frightening Ben-gal himself, though the latter wouldn't admit it. And all over a telephone. And the call coming from somewhere *inside* Israel. Ben-gal hadn't bothered to put a trace on it because he'd assumed the order to have come from Carmel himself. Now it would take weeks to find its origin.

Sefer had disobeyed him. Why? Because he was afraid of the broadcast? Afraid Carmel couldn't handle it? Afraid for the dikes of northern Europe? Hell, he had the *names* now; he could handle it. He could handle much more. Damn the bearded Englishman!

Carmel summons the Iraqi.

"Go out and pick up Kazin. Put a tail on Berman and Selliger as well as a girl in Jerusalem named Wallinchek, Zilpah Wallinchek. And have Kazin brought to *me*. You know where." He pauses for a moment, then snaps his fingers. "As for that Austrian, call Pnina in Vienna and have her tail him. If he moves east, tell her she can shoot."

The Iraqi is surprised.

"Are you sure she should do that? Remember, in Norway—"

"That was over two years ago. People forget."

He sighs wearily, then picks up the telephone, dialing the Jerusalem Police. He'd need a full guard at the radio station tonight; nobody in the broadcast who's not allowed. He'd find Wand, all right. He'd learn his name if he had to kill him.

"Understood?"

Carmel cannot wait to see Kazin.

The pleasure is nearly equal to his anger. Sefer, that bearded, meddling Englishman! Damn him!

20

Gad has awakened with a sore throat. (Lingering guilts? he asks himself.) He crosses to the bathroom and runs the tub water. According to the schedule arranged with Sefer, Gad is to start to work on the crystal one hour before the broadcast. Sefer will have placed the sister crystal on the BBC transmitter. Gad will then try to put it out of commission in three intervals of three minutes apiece.

He will then have forty-some minutes to get to the studio, to enter it, to locate the psychics and to begin defusing them.

He promises himself a vacation afterward. Somewhere in the sun with Gwyneth. Thinking of her, he retrieves the scarf and carries it to the bathtub. Before stepping into the water, he holds it tightly, straining.

Slowly Gwyneth begins to appear. Below a cliff near the sea. In a storm. Something to do with a circle. There are others beside her. He can perceive two other forms. It feels odd, but not dangerous.

He drops the scarf onto the floor and steps into the bath.

21

Sefer stands before the BBC signal tower. It would be simple to place the crystal at its base, then to leave. But to have the crystal at the center of the signal dish, surely that would be the ideal position.

He moves to the other side of the tower, where the metal ladder had been soldered into place. He hates heights, hates physical exertion. He looks back at the watchman sprawled in the grass. He hadn't done him too much harm, poor man. As long as the watchman lay there like a good fellow, Sefer could pop up the ladder and be at the dish in a matter of minutes.

Joseph Sefer takes a deep breath, puts the crystal in his pocket and begins to climb. The other guard isn't due for an hour.

22

Hurriedly depositing their luggage in the house of the
taciturn Frøken Agda, Gwyneth and her friends have
surprised the old woman by turning out once again
into the storm. They were agreed upon the setting for the
ceremony as soon as they had seen the spot: a cliff facing the
northeastern portion of the planet.

The lava makes their climbing difficult, for it is jagged from
birth, slippery from the gathering rain, jet-black and inhospita-
ble. Below them, the sea boils and churns beneath the black
lowering clouds. They say nothing, continuing to move slowly,
solemnly above the sleeping village and toward an outcrop
that faces the direction necessary to their work.

Astrud points to the right. Far into the deep of the yellow-
black sea and sky, a Danish ship is tossing. One flare, then
two seem to explode from its decks. Mayday, the distress call,
has been sent out continuously from the radio. The three
women spot the sailors and hope their ceremony will in some
way help the men through the tossing ocean's bulk.

"There," says Lisaveta, looking up. Before them a flat plot
of land slopes evenly toward the cliff, its natural curvature
protecting it from southwesterly winds. Gwyneth glances back
at the village. Certainly they are far enough away to defy obser-

vation. She turns to the others, nodding. Astrud deposits the bag she'd been carrying onto a lava bulge. This will serve them as an altar.

Lisaveta takes the ground chalk from the bag, counting off twelve feet from the altar, then kneels. She begins to pour the chalk in a large circle, until three feet remain open. Eventually she will close this area as well. But not yet. It is too soon.

Gwyneth takes a vial of water and pours it into the small silver calyx Lisaveta has provided. She sets it at the western quarter of the circle. Astrud begins to remove several dried plants from her mac pocket—impatiens, clematis, moon rose—and sets them in a copper dish. Into the dish she mixes nine drops of oil of bergamot. Then she lights the mixture. The tiny offering sputters, sparks, and an overwhelmingly sensual scent begins to lift into the air. Astrud places the dish at the eastern quarter of the circle. Almost magically, the storm subsides.

Lisaveta reaches into the bag for the thick violet wax candle, then sets the tin shield with the arcane markings around it. She lights the wick, placing the shielded candle at the southern quarter. Finally, Gwyneth brings out a large quartz crystal from the bag, placing it on a piece of silver-colored silk. This she sets at the northern quarter of the circle, then turns to Astrud and Lisaveta. The latter closes up the rest of the circle with the chalk.

They are ready. Standing within the magic plot.

Under no condition will they leave the circle until the ceremony has ended.

Lisaveta takes the oil of bergamot, applying it to her forehead—then to Gwyneth's, to Astrud's. She puts a drop at the pulse point of her right and left hands, repeating the gesture with the other women.

It is time.

The three stand around the altar in a tight circle, placing

158

their pulse points together, Gwyneth's against Lisaveta's and Astrud's. They raise their arms in the air. Lisaveta begins the slow chant:

"Ateh malkuth ve-geburah ve-gedulah, le olam. . . . Amen. . . ."

Their upraised arms begin to sway, designing into the ether a six-pointed star. They lower their arms below the altar.

"Ateh malkuth ve-geburah ve-gedulah, le olam. . . . Amen. . . ."

Designing the star of six points.

They turn to the east.

"Ateh malkuth. . . ."

Now Gwyneth must furnish the pentacles of protection at each quadrant. She feels a surge of energy at the base of her spine and slowly begins to raise her right hand, drawing a five-pointed star into the ether.

Astrud claps her hands slowly, thrice.

Gwyneth turns to the south, repeating the formula for the foundation of the pentacles. Then to the west and finally to the north.

Astrud starts to laugh, pointing toward the north with glittering familiarity. "Uriel is approaching," she whispers, and Lisaveta nods. Sure enough, the northern portion of the circle seems to have gathered around it a dense and tension-filled force, a force beginning to respond to the intention of the ceremony.

Lisaveta holds her hands toward the sea until her fingertips are tingling.

> *Nescio quis sim*
> *Nescio unde veniam*
> *Nescio quo eam.*
>> *Quaero*
> *Sed quid nescio . . .*

Gwyneth, Astrud and Lisaveta clap their hands nine times, then turn toward the crystal upon the silvery scarf. It has begun to glow as if it contained a myriad of diamonds, flashing and sparkling, developing a cold flame to penetrate the atmosphere.

"Non accedet ad me malum. . . ."

It is as if the circle had started to tilt, drawn to the north, Uriel's corner, and was sucking them toward it. Even the flame at the southern quarter is veering to the north. A force, gathering itself steeply, mightily is beginning to rise. Gwyneth holds her arms out, northward, chanting:

"O Uriel, Guardian and Protector of the kingdoms of water, show yourself in an image most pleasing. Know we are of Beauty, of the Sphere of Tiphereth. Know that Sandalphon and Metatron protect us. Know of the pentacles we have placed around us, of the six-pointed stars above and below this circle of intent. O Force of Uriel, potent northern charge, show yourself in an image most pleasing to our sight."

Astrud's teeth have begun to chatter, as much from the cold now emanating from the northern aspect of the circle as from her own excitement. Instinctively she reaches for the ceremonial dagger on the altar, the blade of protection. It isn't there. She has forgotten. In their studies, as a magical trine, Lisaveta had become the blade, her aura sharp and cutting. Gwyneth had become the wand, intense and forceful, clear in her purpose. Astrud herself, knowledgeable in the language of the forest, subtle and dangerous as a leopard, had learned the protective vocabulary of the pentacle. Together, as a trine, they formed the feminine cup, deep and receptive, gathering and binding, creating and destroying.

Lisaveta and Gwyneth clap their hands nine times once again.

"Show yourself," Gwyneth repeats. "In the name of the Ain, the Eternal, the Idea above the Crown, above Kether, we command you, Uriel!"

Lisaveta plants her feet wide apart, bracing herself for the appearance of the force. Gwyneth leans forward slightly, her hair whipping about her features, eyes transfixed above and slightly beyond the crystal. Slowly she moves her left arm up-

160

ward, stretching it toward the clouds. Then she shoots out her right arm.

She has lost nothing. The force within her is as potent as it was ten years ago.

Astrud shudders at the peal of thunder.

Lisaveta looks heavenward, frowning.

But Gwyneth does not move. At the northern edge of the circle, beyond the crystal, an Idea has been summoned, given force, and is now assuming form. The crystal appears to be burning.

Lisaveta shivers as the northern energy tries to fight its way into the circle, to surround the women, to blast them into the sea. A natural force is being summoned unnaturally, forced to perform an action against its own natural movement. The intelligence within that force is causing it to rebel.

"Show yourself!" screams Gwyneth. "In the name of the All-Knowing, we call you!"

Then Astrud feels it, force-fully, and curls like an autumn leaf to the ground.

Instinctively Lisaveta touches Gwyneth's shoulder, beginning to move toward the north, sensing the electrical tug. Gwyneth grabs her friend, pulling her back. Both hold out their right hands as if they contained electrical wands. Both say, "In the name of the All-Knowing. . . ."

And it takes form: its height incalculable, its breadth immeasurable. A column of crystal-blue light stretching into the heavens. And beside it, around it, vague forms begin to shape themselves in myriad clusters, droplets of ice, faces frozen in ice, yet moving constantly, rushing about the column of Uriel as bees around a peculiarly potent flower. Behind them, humming, sparks give off electrical heat, aspects of the borealis in human shape, a woman made of frozen sunlight, her ice-hair hanging to her knees, and a castle stretching to blackness, icy forms of winged horses carrying death-blue warriors toward a darkened archway, the archway shifting rapidly to form the

161

vulva of a winter goddess, deep-blue her breath and crackling the lightning glow of her eyes, the breath sucking them close to the northern edge of the circle, into her, to become beings of her, and the column constantly compounding, building methodically, moving higher, the humming broad and steady as the ice-bound goddess beckons and Lisaveta moves toward the crystal beam. Again, Gwyneth catches her.

"Name yourself!" she commands, and the column nods slowly, trying to penetrate the circle, to move toward them, to blow them off the face of the cliff. But it cannot penetrate the circle. "We are of Tiphereth, the Sphere of Beauty," Gwyneth continues. "Protected by the force of Raphael, calling in the name of the Ain, we demand you swear your allegiance to our task and to our aim!"

The column rises mightily, attempting to cover them in a cold whose end is death.

Gwyneth's arm remains pointed at the column. An invisible wand at work.

23

Gad takes the crystal which Sefer has given him and sets it on the table. Sefer has told him only one thing: to imagine the crystal reaching out to connect it with the other crystal, the one set at the transmitter, and to charge the invisible line between them with a constant stream of electrical sparks. To bombard it.

Gad sighs, takes a breath, exhaling long and steadily, then begins to let the sparks fly.

Gad waits, listening. Something is wrong. There is too much movement beyond the sparking.

He closes his eyes and finds himself standing beside the BBC signal dish. Everything crackles about him as in a dream. His own motion is off; his movements seem jerky. He forces himself to look down, to fight the crackling in his ears. He sees Sefer moving. Spots the guard grip his service revolver with both hands, then watches as the guard exhales, slowly, carefully, consciously, and squeezes the trigger.

Gad sees Sefer appearing to spin off the tower as if it were the simplest circus trick, to somersault three times in midair before landing. And the guard turning away, giving himself up to nausea. Giving himself to pain.

163

Gad screams soundlessly, returning to the room in Israel. His shock transforms to hatred and to fear.

The signal dish is glowing. Then it begins to burn. The universe is alive with searing, imploding metal. A face the size of the Postal Tower appears above the dish: a young man with silvery hair, with clear and hateful eyes now glowing red with vengeance.

His own ears pop from the shrieking.

24

The black clouds dissolve on the western horizon. A slim pink sky shows below the violet recesses of the approaching night. The Uriel Column has departed, moving steadily toward the face of northern Europe, to lie as a freezing blanket upon the waves.

Tomorrow meteorologists will be surprised by the cold spell. It will come too soon, too early. No prediction will foresee the extent of that strange and solemn spell.

Gwyneth, Lisaveta and Astrud stand at the edge of the cliff, watching the ice-blue form move farther east like a whale, over the waters, over the waves. The stars above their heads take the form of a crown and seem to leap and dance in their hair.

Astrud is yawning; Lisaveta, too.

Gwyneth picks up the bag beside the rock and starts to move down to the village.

"I'd forgotten the power," she says, taking Astrud by the arm. "Poor darling. . . ."

The Brazilian is pale, but smiles wryly. "Next time, come

to Brazil, to the *Mato Grosso,*" she says. "Your turn to faint. . . ."

Gwyneth looks back toward the cliff, her face wet, features slightly pinched from the frost.

"I'm starving," says Lisaveta. "Let's hope the old woman has some hot soup."

But Gwyneth is elsewhere. She frowns and presses Astrud's hand. Her friend looks up, surprised.

"What is it?"

Astrud glances at Lisaveta, who has stooped to pick the brilliant orange crown off an ice plant. Astrud frowns. "Gwyn, what's wrong?"

"Nothing," whispers Gwyneth. "I just . . . thought of something."

"What?"

But Gwyneth shakes her head once again. They continue to move swiftly down to the village.

The dark and winding lane leading to the central row of houses is but fifty meters before them.

25

In the last cell of an ancient slaughterhouse, Carmel stands before Kazin. The latter, in suit and tie, looks comically disgruntled, like some petit bourgeois out for a night at the theater and surprised to find himself dumped unceremoniously in a mudhole.

Carmel wastes no time. "It is our understanding you are part of a network attempting to subvert the State of Israel."

Kazin doesn't blink. He isn't the least bit shocked. "I only hope you have proof," he replies flatly.

"Oh, we've proof. Todi blew it open. We've all the proof we need."

Kazin licks his lips, his eyes traveling to the concrete floor and to the drainhole in its center. What is it for?

"We know all about the psychics," Carmel continues. "Selliger, Berman and that girl. Rest assured, the radio broadcast is a point of major interest. Who's your man in the East?"

Kazin says nothing.

"Good," Carmel smiles, turning to the Iraqi. "Failing to comply with the request of an officer?"

The Iraqi nods.

Carmel slaps Kazin harshly, twice, across the face. "I'm going

167

to ask you once again, Kazin. Then I'm going to take you apart. You know who I am, don't you?"

Kazin shakes his head.

"My name is Eli Carmel."

Kazin's mouth goes tight. Then he spits in Carmel's face. Carmel doesn't bother to wipe the spittle from his collar. His punch is delivered with such force that his knuckles ache.

"The name," he hisses, then snaps his fingers to the Iraqi. The latter tosses him a switchblade. Kazin, against the wall, stares at it fearfully.

"Jira," he whispers. "Dr. Jira."

"And where is Jira?"

"In Prague."

"Thank you," says Carmel, ramming the weapon deep into Kazin's throat. "Send the prick back to his Czech friends," he barks and, turning, leaves the cell.

26

Oliver Gad moves idly before the artists' entrance of the radio station, watching the guards take the identification cards from the musicians. The broadcasting area itself is ringed with police.

Gad looks back at Ilse in the bar across the street and frowns. How to enter the station? He is afraid of projecting himself, afraid he hasn't the strength. The bursting of the BBC signal tower has drained him, and the sight of Sefer lying like a gutted fish. In his fury, seeing Sefer killed, he'd released his Astral Ape. He'd come to like Sefer, damn him, and where was he now? Dead at the base of a tower. When Gad had emerged from the bedroom, Ilse's eyes had gone wide.

"What is it?" she had asked, frightened by his look. "What has happened?"

He had stared at her without seeing her, without seeing anything.

Everything had gone so well, had been so damned easy. And now Sefer was dead, for something as stupid as a night climb on a tower.

Gad stands at the corner wondering what to do when a busload of refugees pulls up to the artists' door. He moves closer, trying to catch sight of Asher, Selliger and that girl. But it is too dark.

Then the obvious solution comes to him, and he curses himself.

Moving behind the group, he dematerializes one of several cards from the hand of the policeman and presents it back to him.

"Shalom," says the guard.

Oliver smiles and holds up two fingers in a victory sign. Quickly he enters the station.

A honey-haired, gray-eyed girl-soldier leads them through a back corridor and into a theater. Gad lets himself be directed toward the makeshift bleachers before the orchestra. The musicians themselves are present onstage and are tuning up. Gad senses at once the dark, intense young man seated at the pianoforte, playing a series of chromatic scales: Joseph Selliger.

One down, two to go, thinks Gad, gazing around once again. But he cannot find Asher Berman among the excited faces of the participants. A commotion causes him to turn, then to freeze.

Eli Carmel is moving from the control booth angrily, shouting orders at two men. With a rage that instantly sets him apart from the others, Carmel strides directly to Selliger and lifts the young man's hands from the keyboard.

"Asher Berman," he spits. "Where is he?"

Selliger is surprised. "I don't know."

"What do you mean you don't know?"

Selliger looks around for support. Who is this man?

"He didn't come back last night. I thought he'd be here. Anyway, he's crazy."

Gad rises, and Carmel looks up. Their eyes meet. Carmel turns once again to the confused Selliger. "Where did he go?"

Gad begins to move closer to the pair, snatching a page of music from the violinist and pretending to read it.

"He was with a girl," Joseph snaps petulantly. "Some American."

170

Carmel is puzzled.

"American?"

Joseph sighs. "He said they wanted him to go to America, to make records."

Now Hirsch, the conductor, is moving toward the pair and puts a protective hand on Selliger's shoulder.

"Please, what is going on?"

Carmel grabs Selliger by the arm and lifts him off the piano stool.

"Hey. . . !"

"Come with me," he snaps. To Hirsch: "Won't be a minute."

Gad watches them move to a corner of the studio, then follows. Selliger is terrified.

"Dr. Jira," says Carmel. "Do you know him?"

Selliger shakes his head.

"Did Asher Berman know him?"

Selliger nods. "Jira's a she. That's what Asher said."

"What did she do to you?"

"Nothing. I don't *know* her!" says Selliger, his voice rising half an octave.

Carmel nods. A baby. A pampered child.

"Where is the girl, Zilpah Wallinchek?"

Selliger frowns. "I don't know."

"She was also in Prague?"

"How do I know? I was never in Prague. Maybe Asher was. *He's* the lover. . . ." Selliger hates Asher now, intensely, irrationally. This is all Asher's doing, all Asher's fault. His *own* moment of triumph, and Asher by his absence is wrecking it.

"All right," says Carmel. "Be calm. I am sorry to have disturbed you. . . ."

The Iraqi whistles. Carmel looks up. The man points to some chorus members who have entered the theater and are moving toward the bleachers. An attractive young girl with flaming red hair is talking excitedly with her companion. Gad sees her as well. More, he spots the bracelet on her wrist identical to the one Selliger is wearing. Immediately Gad steps forward, planting himself between Carmel and the girl.

"Couldn't help overhearing," he begins, terribly British. "If you're looking for Berman, I think I can find him."

"Fifteen minutes," says a voice over the loudspeaker.

"Who are you?" asks Carmel.

"I am Wand," the young man replies, and his smile is bitter but effective.

27

Gwyneth Powys sits in the drawing room of the guest-house, fiddling with the radio dial.

"Surely we should receive the BBC," she wonders. Lisaveta translates the question into Danish. The old woman nods, pointing to a number. Gwyneth moves aside as Lisaveta begins turning the dial. After a moment she says, "Nothing but static."

Gwyneth smiles. "Good," and flicks off the switch.

In the performance of magic, Intention is all.

The Intention of the Elementals is to destroy and to shape, to replenish and to nurture, to alter energy to matter, matter to energy. The psychic alchemy of the Elementals is constant and as distinct from man's nature as a sun's from a grasshopper's. Thus, for a human entity to draw upon the Elementals for a specific end is to ask them to align their own nature to man's, to move in a direction and toward an end contrary to their own.

The northern form which Gwyneth had conjured had been in rebellion. But the pentacles she had set into the ether were signs of protection and of knowledge. Gwyneth's understanding of the six-pointed stars connected her with the wisdom of civilizations long dead and yet to form. The Elementals had to obey, for the force emanating from Gwyneth was of a potency and of an Intention none of them possessed.

The battle of wills was over. Gwyneth had won. But on another plane of existence, intersecting with and yet apart from man's, the extent of Gwyneth's *force* had become known, for her magical act had opened the door to the Astral Plane; named and naked, the Gwyneth spirit had begun to vibrate among the forces of that dimension.

As soon as Gwyneth and Lisaveta demanded allegiance from the power of Uriel, the Northern Force, the spirit of Leila Kent began to stir.

28

Oliver Gad holds the bracelets in both hands and closes his eyes. For a moment all is darkness. Then a range of mountains appears. The sea. He hears voices, laughter. He looks around in his mind's eye, sees an automobile with blue-and-yellow California license plates and two people moving luggage into a low-slung ranch house.

"California," he says. "Berman's in California."

Carmel shakes his head wearily. "Are you certain?"

"Of course I'm certain," Gad snorts. "Would Sefer have picked a fool?"

Carmel's eyes narrow. That accent should have told him. When they had stared at each other, he should have recognized the young man as one of the passengers on the plane. How in hell had he managed to sneak into the theater?

"Your Mr. Sefer is extremely independent and inconsiderate."

"Was," says Gad, quietly, and Carmel seems to feel the floor rise up to meet him. He stands, legs apart, leaning slightly against the wall.

"What is this?" he whispers.

"He appears to have been shot at the BBC transmitter."

"How do you know?"

"I know."

Carmel struggles within himself. After a moment his sense of reason puts sentiment and depth of feeling in its place. It is a question of survival, isn't it? Isn't it always?

"Give them back their bracelets," he says hoarsely.

Gad shakes his head. "On the condition I stand beside them during the concert."

Carmel hates him. Irrationally he feels somehow that Gad is connected with Sefer's death. Gad senses his irritation and the danger within it.

"Watch," he says, holding the bracelets out toward Carmel and smiling as they disappear.

"Now reach into your pocket."

Carmel does so. Pulling out the bracelets.

"I'm very polite," Gad counters. *"Please* may I stand beside them? We owe it to our mutual friend."

Carmel nods, saying nothing. Gad takes the bracelets, returns them to their owners. Zilpah is made to sit near the pianist, within five feet of Gad. A chair is brought to the Englishman and placed beside Selliger.

Gad closes his eyes once again, trying to force Asher's bracelet to materialize, his link to California. But nothing happens. Nothing is happening.

Perhaps I'm too tired, he thinks. Perhaps the distance is too far.

Hirsch taps his baton against the podium.

The musicians straighten.

The concert is about to begin.

Asher Berman screams, but no sound emerges. Instead, all the windows in the house shatter.

"Earthquake!" yells Celia, but the house is not swaying, the ground not trembling. Beyond the broken window, a couple on horseback and riding at the cliff's edge gaze dreamily toward the Pacific.

Asher is white and clutching crazily at his bracelet to force it off his hand; Celia stares at him helplessly.

"Jesus, Asher . . ." she whines. "Jesus Christ. . . ." The doors blow open; the glasses begin to smash; the lamps fall crashing from their stands.

"Asher," she moans, clutching at him, but his misery is not to be shared.

The power beam comes in waves, in undulations that grow in strength, similar to the pounding of the Atlantic in a winter's storm. Gad feels it at once, the shock of it pulsing from the base of his spine to the crown of his head. His hands grip the wrists of Joseph and Zilpah. He fights to keep them there, pressing hard upon the bracelets until he thinks he will break their wrists. Zilpah is yelling, fighting to wrench herself free, and when several of the orchestra members approach, Gad screams, "Don't touch them!," gritting his teeth, planting his feet squarely on the ground, trying to bring the force down from his head, out through his hands, angry enough to shove it back through the bracelets to the invisible connection some-where in Eastern Europe, to a place where technicians are gathered around odd-looking equipment before an enormous signal dish.

Gad had seen the unmistakable grimace on Selliger's face, had noted the pianist's hands curling over the keys like a chick-en's foot; it was then he'd grabbed their wrists, clamping down on them as Zilpah began to swoon, but he'd caught her in time, and the concert had come to a halt. Hirsch and the techni-cians had started to move toward the trio, but Carmel ordered them back, shouting to the controls engineer to keep the pro-gram *live,* to keep the signal on the air, and Gad had felt the horrible shock of the connection ripping into his gut.

His legs are trembling, knees knocking together like casta-nets, but he holds on. For Sefer's sake. For his own. Then everyone begins to scream as subsidiary phenomena sweep through the theater like an invisible tidal wave: The piano wires snap; bows bend; kettle drum keys melt; tapes in the control booth start spinning of their own accord, snapping off the reels. The monitor bank has begun to smoke, and finally, the glass panel of the control booth which separates engineer from cast shatters inward, the shards blinding one of the technicians.

It is confusion, it is chaos, but Gad holds on. Selliger has struck his head on the edge of the keyboard and is bleeding profusely above his right eye; Zilpah is trying to claw and scratch at Gad's hand, but he will not let go, he can't, forcing that current back from his head down to the base of his spine, then out through the nerves of his hands and into the bracelets, drawing upon their own energy now, feeling it draining out, slowly, to travel elsewhere, slowly; and he is saying to Joseph, "All right, are you all right?" and then to Zilpah, "Are you all right?" but they can only stare, bug-eyed and frozen.

Then he hears the snap. Sees an enormous sheet of white fire. Then he releases their wrists.

"There," he says, and straightens his coat. "You may remove the bracelets now. . . ."

Carmel is staring at Gad as if he had walked on water.

Gad smiles vaguely, tossing the Israeli the bracelets. With an absurd grin, he crumples to the floor.

PART
THREE

*And may not I such power upon me take,
without disdain or spite?*

—Ovid, *Metamorphoses,* Book X

1

D r. Jira is a most unhappy woman.

The communication has been set carefully before her. She feels it will prove an albatross: *Suggest you locate third party immediately and terminate all links.* She has chosen silence as a response, if only to assure herself of the reality of the albatross. Within twenty-four hours three KGB officials have appeared. Wondrous assurance! But of what? The reality of her masochism?

There is no end to it, she thinks. My work is being proved dispensable. And yet what *did* go wrong with Asher Berman? Surely there had been adequate enough programming, at least to hold him in Israel.

"Dr. Jira," one of the officials is saying, "Please let us have your full attention."

"Simple enough for a saint to do," she replies. "Or someone fighting for her life."

They do not smile. The aphorism, characteristically Czech, means nothing to them.

"We are presenting you with two choices: either to retrieve Berman and to destroy him, or to face proceedings in Russia."

Dr. Jira nods pleasantly. "Inasmuch as I protested the length of time given me to work with Berman, I am convinced of the outcome. . . ."

The KGB officer shrugs. "Very well. We will leave for Russia this evening."

"Therefore," continues Dr. Jira, "I will retrieve Asher Berman. Wherever he may be."

Jira keeps the men waiting in her office and crosses to the laboratory. Sârka, the young woman with the round-rimmed spectacles, is holding the copper bracelet.

"Am I correct?" asks Jira with uncharacteristic impatience.

Sârka writes something on a piece of paper, handing it to the doctor. Then she passes the bracelet to Vasla, the blond, moon-faced assistant. Vasla runs a magnet across the bracelet, ridding it of the electromagnetic patterns of Sârka's thoughts, removing any impregnations the other worker may have left upon it.

Jira watches her assistants lethargically, but smiles as Vasla's face brightens and as she also writes several words on a piece of paper.

Jira takes the slips and opens them.

So I am right, she thinks. Both girls reply simultaneously, "Asher Berman. United States. Southern California."

"Sârka?" She smiles, and the thin young woman with the round spectacles glances up anxiously. Her will is extraordinary, thinks Jira. Such tenacity. The stuff of nuns. Poor Sârka. She has to work at what Vasla does naturally, unthinkingly. How long will her innocence last?

"Vasla?"

The girl with the wheat-colored hair looks up as well. Both watch Jira, trying to divine her thoughts, but Jira has set a shield about her aura that only a Mage could penetrate.

"Would you care to come with me to Southern California?"

Suddenly the girls are shrieking, clapping their hands. Jira silences them with the raising of an eyebrow. "If so, you must tell me: Where in Southern California will we find Asher Berman?"

Sârka turns worriedly to Vasla, who replies, "Los Angeles."
"Is that correct, Sârka?"
Sârka nods cautiously. Jira tousles her hair, tweaks her on the nose.
"You must learn to not force yourself, Sârka. You must learn to relax. Of course he is in Los Angeles. And with the three of us, we will certainly find him."
"But then," says Sârka, frowning still, "what will we do? Are you going to let us—"
"First let us find him. Then let us discover how his electromagnetic field evaded the program."
"The Russians forced—"
"No," Jira interrupts, holding out her hand and toying with Vasla's hair for the pleasure of its wheaty softness. "We accepted the forcing. We therefore did the forcing ourselves. The problem, I fear, is that we allowed ourselves to be programmed by the Russians' own concerns. I trust we will be beyond that, all of us, in Los Angeles."
She starts to return to her office, but Sârka waves at her like a schoolgirl. "Doctor? How did the wave get sent back to Russia?"
Jira smiles. Jira shrugs.
"A wonderful question. And one which could well be answered in Southern California."

"Gentlemen," she begins, and the officials rise at the tone of authority in her voice. "I will need three visas to America. Three airplane tickets to Los Angeles. Please tell your superiors that we will attend to their request. Tell your superiors that we will think of them as brothers."
The KGB men nod curtly.
"Very well, Dr. Jira," the leading officer replies dryly, to Jira's amusement. "I am sure they will be happy to know you still feel the ties of such a brotherly relationship."
Jira nods, thinking: And why are these lumpheads our brothers? Because who picks family?

2

For the rest of the evening following the broadcast Oliver Gad has been kept in the quarantine ward of the Hadassah Hospital, guarded by the Iraqi.

The following morning Carmel appears with the doctor.

"Well?" Gad begins weakly from the bed. "And where are we now?"

While the doctor examines him, Carmel hands Oliver the *Jerusalem Post.*

Front-page photo of the North Sea. The North European shoreline, from Rotterdam to Hamburg, frozen. Waves locked in motion. A photographer's dream of the Apocalypse. And with it, a cold spell throughout Europe, totally unexpected and out of season.

"Surprising news, eh?" says Carmel. "In spite of your help, look what the Sovs accomplished."

"Sovs, indeed," snorts Gad. "The Gwyn's been up and about."

But Carmel isn't listening. "Unfortunately," he continues, "I've not been able to get through to our mutual friend Mr. Sefer, so I can't tell if your guess about his condition's correct."

Gad shakes his head slowly.

"Of course it's correct," he counters. "Stupid fool. . . ."

Carmel sighs. "We're working on Selliger and that girl, trying to walk them through their moments with the Prague doctor. But neither of them seems to be able to recollect anything about Prague. And as for Berman, he's disappeared."

Gad closes his eyes thoughtfully while Carmel continues: "You might be interested to know there's been an earthquake in Uzbek, in southern Russia. The reports haven't arrived yet in detail, but last night we picked up the Rumanian and Turkish broadcasts. It appears you sent the monster right back to their laps." The news holds slight interest for Gad. He bares his backside while the doctor administers a potent dose of vitamin complex.

"This Prague doctor," Gad begins. "What do you know about him?"

Carmel smiles dryly. "First, he is a she. A most respected she. From what we've gathered, her husband, Viktor, was one of the leading physicists after the war. He became interested in parapsychology, specifically those physical laws governing paraphysical phenomena. Tragically, one of his sponsors was Slansky. During the postwar purge he was executed."

"The Stalin era?"

"Of course. Jira's wife must have been quite young then. She wasn't allowed to continue his work. What she did after her husband's death we do not know for certain. Mind you, that's nearly fifteen years of silence."

"You don't have a clue?"

"One of our reports states she worked in a hospital as a nurse. In Bratislava. Another says she traveled and spent several years in Mongolia."

"Curious reports."

"No, the latter is quite possible. Viktor Jira's initial work in parapsychology was a physical study of the ecstatic state of the Mongol shamans. Perhaps she had contacts there, who knows? Then she began to emerge under Dubček and was fully reinstated or at least surfaced when Husak took over. Perhaps you cannot enjoy the irony, but Husak also had been purged with Slansky, London and Jira. But he survived. Our

185

lady is also a survivor. We'll learn a great deal more about her soon enough."

"Dr. Jira," whispers Gad, as if the name were a magical mantra. "By the way, do you have the bracelets?"

"Of course. Why?"

Gad frowns.

"Do you think the bracelets are still active, Mr. Gad?"

But Gad shakes his head. "Not without Selliger and that damned girl wearing them." His arms and cheeks still smart from Zilpah's fingernails. "But Berman's still wearing *his,* and any psychometrist worth his *Abra* will know where Berman's gone. For myself I don't even know the man, but last night I saw he was in California. I'm sure he's there still. I'm sure this Dr. Jira must know it as well. . . . I'd certainly like to meet her."

Carmel nods. "Berman took TWA Flight eight forty-two, Athens-Rome-New York, the night before last, and with an interim American passport. You're quite right, Mr. Gad. Our people in America have traced him to Los Angeles. But where's he staying, that's the question. He didn't seem to be traveling with anybody."

Gad snorts: "Gone or not, he still has the bracelet, which means he's still smoking. I'd like to get to him before Jira does."

Carmel frowns. "What?"

"I can assure you she'll try to get Berman." Then, as if to himself: "Jira . . . Dr. Jee-ra. . . ."

Carmel glances at the doctor impatiently. "When can he leave the hospital?"

"Whenever he wants," replies the man. "I'm not very happy about his metabolic rate, though the change is to be expected."

Gad shrugs, gazing amusedly at the doctor. "Quite. Well, then, I shall leave for the States immediately, if it's at all possible."

Carmel nods. "Certainly."

"And on expenses? After all, with my own man out of commission. . . ."

"Naturally."

"And I must do things my own way. . . ."

Carmel dismisses the doctor, then turns to Gad, leaning across the bed. "Have you ever done anything differently?" he whispers.

Gad closes his eyes, lying back on the pillow.

"Sefer's being gone now, it makes no sense. I haven't even begun to assimilate it yet." Then, oddly: "Maybe Jira can teach me something. By the by, what time is it in London?"

"Five in the morning, five-fifteen. And what you think of Sefer is still conjecture."

"As Berman is conjecture in California?" snaps Gad. Then: "I'd like to stop in London first."

"But if Berman's in trouble. . . ."

Gad shakes his head angrily. "I've a generator in London. If Jira's there, I'll be needing all the help I can get." He feels Gwyneth's silken scarf beneath the sheets. "For my metabolic rate," he adds, looking blankly at Carmel. He'd better warn Ilse of his departure. "And now may I use the telephone?"

"Certainly," says Carmel, looking back at Gad equally blankly.

Oliver catches the tone at once.

Why waste a good Israeli contact, he thinks, in Ilse Doyle? God only knows what Carmel will do with her once he discovers the link. For poor old Sefer's sake, forget the thought.

"Skip it," he says, and secretly laughs at the momentary tension in Carmel's eyes. "I'll just skip it, eh, Carmel? What say?"

"As you wish," mutters the Israeli.

"Indeed," sings the Silver Fox, tossing back the top sheet.

"Don't be cocky, Mr. Gad." Carmel's expression is so sad, so intensely human that for the moment Gad can sense the man's murderous past, present and, without a doubt, his future. "Take it from someone who's been in the field a bit longer."

Gad begins to dress impatiently. But still, he is listening.

"After what you did last night, be prepared to find yourself dealing with a wounded and therefore dangerous animal."

"Right," adds the Fox. "And they make the most interesting teachers."

187

3

Celia Graves lies beside the sleeping Asher, watching him vaguely, smoking a cigarette. Her house might well have been condemned as a disaster area, but one phone call to a cleaning service and the subsequent repair work of the builders themselves had put an end to the three minutes of pure terror she'd endured. The thing was weird, terrifically weird, actually kind of wonderful because it was so scary. She'd get a song out of it yet, as she'd told the still shaken Asher. Weakly, he had nodded.

"You must call it 'California Glances,' White Goddess. Every moment someone smiles at you, a disaster occurs. When you look into my eyes, my pants tumble to the floor. When in a dream you take my hand, all the hairs fall off my head. And when you give me a kiss, you find yourself spitting out my teeth. With such a love, what will become of us?"

Celia had laughed, the way he had a taste for disaster, the absurdity of it.

Asher himself couldn't explain what had happened. He had said that his wrist ached, so Celia removed the bracelet, to his feeble protests, and placed the ugly thing on her nightstand. All she knew, all she could remember was that it was as if some Fury had taken possession of the house. She'd even brought in a friend from Topanga who was active in the arcane. He'd dowsed the house, said, "Good vibes," and left.

Celia shudders involuntarily, then puts out the cigarette. She is feeling nauseous, tingling. She reaches into the drawer of the nightstand and brings out an Empire snuffbox. Opens it and whiffs a pinch of the white powder deep into her nostrils. No clear. No jolt. Nothing. The nausea continues.

She brings her feet into half lotus and closes her eyes, trying to control the flow of her breath. She begins to sweat and fights the panicky sensation that her breath is controlling her at a pace and into a dimension beyond her control and conjuration.

"O Mother," she whispers, "Great Mother, this is your daughter, begging. . . ."

The Void through which she intuits the Great Mother, the Light of the World, remains a void. But something brooding, stirring and restless hovers beyond the edge of her consciousness. Her spine becomes assaulted by tiny pricks, as if the unknown creature were testing, prodding, searching for an opening.

"Mother, protect me, let me hear your voice. . . ."

Dimly she perceives the sound of laughter.

"Hey, Ash," she whines, and gives the sleeper a kick. He stirs, pulling the covers further over him. "Asher?" she begs. "Hon-nee. . . ?"

Groggily Asher raises his head and blinks. The air journey has come crashing down on him with a rage. His heart seems to be pumping furiously while his thoughts travel in liquidy slow motion.

"How you feeling?" she asks, trying to smile.

Asher smacks his mouth, rubbing the sleep from his eyes. "Two dinosaurs are playing chess on my lungs. What time is it?"

Celia smiles, his voice is so reassuring. "Two in the morning, hon."

"Bojhe moy, Celyuska. . . !"

She grins, feeling brighter now. Feeling better.

189

"Want to take a drive? Want to go for a swim?"

"Let's go dancing," he groans. "Let us have an amusing and instructive conversation about Western Man. What is with you?" He pulls the covers over his head, groaning, "For a Gentile, you are suddenly very Jewish."

"Are you ready to practice tomorrow? The guys can't wait to meet you."

"Yes, they can. . . ."

"No, they can't," she says urgently, feeling the nausea well up again, the prickling of her spine. Shivering, she reaches across the stand for the telephone.

"Hi, Ken, wake you? Listen, I've got Asher here, wanna say hello?"

She turns to Asher, her eyes glowing with a fever Berman recognizes as something beyond drugs. But what is it? What *is* wrong with her? Where to begin? he thinks, and takes the receiver, mumbling, "This woman is out of her mind. Please you must forgive the interruption. . . ."

"Hey, man, that's cool . . ." says the voice at the other end.

"What is *cool?*" asks Asher. Is he talking to yet another crazy?

"She's always stoned, man. Well, you know, like welcome to L.A., have a nice day, that sort of shit."

"I . . . thank you, man," Asher drawls, then passes the receiver to Celia, above the covers.

"Isn't he far-out, Ken?" Celia orders. Dutifully the voice on the other end agrees. Asher takes the phone from her hand, to place it in the cradle. Celia is staring into space, shivering still. It is as if the phone call had never occurred. Asher takes her hand and squeezes it.

"If you make the coffee, I'll make the music."

Gratefully Celia turns to him. And clings.

Celia and Asher spend the rest of the early morning working out the intricacies of a duet, letting their voices move fugually until, with the rising of the sun, they have created a rich and promising tapestry. Which, in her own way, is all Celia Graves

190

is after. And which, in his own way, Asher is after as well.

The affair of his bracelet has become part of the whacky past, transformed into a crazy duet with strings and chorus. The shivering, for Celia, melts away in the morning sun.

4

Oliver Gad has transferred from the El AL Flight to a BEA, London–Los Angeles. He leans against the door of the first-class cabin of the Trident jet, having bribed the stewardess for a glass of Dubonnet; he is feeling the click-tingle of the ice at its edges; idly he gazes at the viscous roll of the liquid, smeary and oddly comforting. It is peculiar, the way people have been staring at him. At first he thinks it is because he is overly fatigued and shows the strain, or perhaps his City notoriety has become headlines once again in his own absence. He's not checked with Boulter for nearly a week. Perhaps his disappearance has been noted in the press.

Yet even the stewardesses on the El AL flight had been more than attentive. He'd rationalized their warm devotion as something perhaps Israeli Security might have said. Then again, thinks Gad, grinning, it might be due to my unnatural metabolism.

In actual fact he is closer to the truth than he realizes, for Gad has begun to emanate a magical field attraction which is causing people to look up and to stare as if he were a sleek and scrappy lion.

Oliver Gad recognizes the lime-green coat, the toss of silken coppery hair against bold shoulders as the passenger enters the plane.

"Excuse me," she says, and Gad moves aside from the doorway, grinning. At once she looks up: "Ollie!" she yells. Gad nods politely, holds out a hand and materializes a long-stemmed and liquidly pink rose.

Two stewardesses and the flight engineer stare astonishedly, then begin to applaud. With a bow, Gad accepts their acknowledgment of his wonder, takes Gwyneth by the arm and escorts her to their seats.

After the stomach-tightening takeoff, Gwyneth says, "I don't know if you've seen the papers."

Gad smiles. "Your witchy work, my Gwyn?"

She nods happily. "Haven't lost a thing, Gaddy. But it was so bitterly cold in London I did feel a touch guilty. Shouldn't last long, though, the spell."

Gad isn't listening; merely watching the movement of her mouth, the full shape of her lips, the sorcery glitter of her eyes. He's missed her so, and feels it now. He can't believe she is sitting beside him. Gwyneth is saying, "And when he took me to the airport, he told me to say—"

But Gad interrupts her. "Who took you, what?"

"Sefer."

Gad is stunned. Perhaps she doesn't know, hasn't learned. The flight will not be so smooth if she doesn't know.

"What do you mean? When you went to Iceland?"

But Gwyneth shakes her head, laughing. "No, Ollie. *Now*. Coming out to Heathrow, just now."

"*Sefer?* But what are you talking about?"

Gwyneth sighs, taking Gad's hand and playing with his fingers, one by one.

"He's not dead, Ollie. He felt it was time to get out from under Carmel's influence; that's why he did it. He knew you'd meet up with him in Israel."

"*What? What are you talking about?*"

A passenger turns around stiffly, but when Gad looks up, the former gazes at the ceiling.

Gwyneth lowers her voice. "His pretending to have been killed."

Gad feels intense relief mixed with an equal part of rage. He'd been had, once again, by the Beard. But how? He'd seen Sefer tumble off the tower. He'd seen him fall.

"You *thought* you saw him fall," Gwyneth whispers.

"So Carmel—"

"Believes he's dead as well."

Ah, and he wants it that way, thinks Gad. Sefer wants to break away from Carmel's control. It's a one-man operation. Sef plays dead. No more operation, and Sefer can use me far beyond Carmel's influence. Probably the breakaway also improves his stature in M15.

"But how did he do it?"

"Quite simple," Gwyneth replies. "As we've always said, Ollie, you're so thoroughly lacking in the creative process, you'd never understand an act of imagination performed for its own sake."

"Rubbish," Gad interrupts. "I was bloody good back there."

"Of course. With real things. But with thought forms, you're an infant. Not to worry, Ollie. That's why you're so powerful. You've no thought forms to interfere."

Gad frowns. I'm a bleeding Magus, he thinks, and this provincial witch dares chastise me.

Gwyneth looks wryly at Gad. "A provincial witch, were she so inclined, could blow you out of this plane in a matter of seconds." But she is smiling. Waiting.

Gad moves deeper into his seat, fuming to himself.

"Your aura's as red as an engine," she grins. "Now listen to me, love, and learn: Our Sef may be slow in appearance, but he's a most imaginative man. His will is ferocious. You're his child, whether you wish to accept it or not."

"But how did he do it? How did he appear to be dead?"

"As I said. With a thought."

Gwyneth sniffs the rose, then tweaks Gad on his cheek with its limp petal.

194

"This rose is real," she begins.

"Of course it is." Oliver glowers. "I only materialize the genuine."

"But so is a thought. It's every bit as tangible, as genuine as this airplane. And on the Astral, it's even *more* genuine."

"Continue," he growls. "And please: what is the *Astral?*"

"Once your sensory range is extended, you'll see it. It's a sort of webbing between the physical plane and the higher planes. It filters higher energies to our plane. Without the filter we couldn't survive. Among other things, the Astral is composed of our private thoughts and the emotions of our deeds. Imagine a drain in which all of humanity's thoughts and deeds are washed. That's the Astral. It's a most cluttered intersection, and quite powerful. We use astral energy all the time, but most of us either are unaware of it or refuse to accept it as a part of our own inner geography. Psychiatrists would have a much easier time dealing with phobias and psychoses if they studied the Astral."

"Give me an example, Dr. Powys."

Gwyneth smiles and puts her head on Gad's shoulder.

"A nightmare is only a thought form," she continues. "Your fear becomes altered on the Astral. Fear, filtered, becomes a demon. And there you are, in the Astral, fighting a demon, while in the physical you're merely confronting your fear. Simultaneous lives, Gaddy-boy."

Oliver nods, frowning. "When I use my psychic abilities—"

"The energy can be Astral. All Sefer did, since he knew you were linked to him through the crystal, was to project a strong thought form of himself falling off the tower. And when you drew your energy from the Astral, when you brought it up, you read his projection and thought it was real."

"But why didn't Sefer tell me?"

"He wanted that transmitter knocked out completely. He knew you'd release the Ape if you thought him killed. He also needed Carmel to think him dead. I believe he wants to turn the game around a bit. After all, who's paying you to go to Los Angeles?"

"Carmel."

"Good. And whatever Carmel's been hiding from Sefer, you yourself, Ollie, are now in a position to discover. As far as Carmel believes, you're not under Sef's control."

Gad nods, intensely relieved. How could he have been so naïve? Sefer is such an admirable bastard.

"What did he want you to tell me?"

Gwyneth turns away and gazes at the stewardess bringing lunch trays to three mean-looking children and a thoroughly anguished mother.

"He's proud of you," she says simply.

"He's proud of himself, you mean," mumbles Gad.

"No," she replies. "He could never do what you've done. He hasn't your concrete abilities. And he says you are brave. I think that's rather nice, don't you?"

Gwyneth is asleep, her head on Gad's shoulder.

Gad himself remains awake, staring out the window, watching the cold patches of the north lying frozen beneath him. He cannot easily forget the lesson Sefer has taught him, the illusionist power of thought, its wretched ability to confound and to confuse. And what other secrets does Sefer possess? Or Gwyneth, for that matter?

Gad feels no wiser than before. The questions still pose themselves with the forthrightness of a cavalry charge.

Why does he do things in threes? Something about creating a power trine, the way the Russians had dealt with Selliger, Wallinchek and Berman?

Then he remembers the cabbalist equation: Idea to Force to Form. The equation of the Creative Act. The magical ceremony.

You have an Idea.

You can't develop it without having Force.

You can't develop it, however great your will, however great your force, without having the proper form.

Gad swims in the possibilities of that simple idea until he threatens to float away. How now to put it into practice?

Then he realizes that it has already taken shape in the Trinity of Sefer-Gwyneth-Gad. And that the Holy Trinity itself, the Father-Mother-Child, the Trinity of all cosmologies, is based upon a *working* knowledge of the equation of Creation: Idea-Force-Form.

Once, he remembers now, and it comes as something of a shock, Sefer had asked him, "Were you ever in Prague?"

What had Sefer known, or was he merely guessing?

Oliver Gad feels a tingling at his wrist. He scratches at the bracelet, the copper one with the quartz crystal that had belonged—how long ago it now seemed—to Joseph Selliger. Carmel had warned him against wearing it, but Gad wants the connection, his link to the West Coast. If the Opposition is to try another show, he'd force the power back through the bracelet though it might kill him. Most of all, he wants to meet the doctor; the bracelet, he knows, is his calling card.

He scratches at his wrist, gazing vaguely below at the icy plain.

"Nice to know," he says, and Gwyneth stirs, mumbling.

"Know what?"

"Know that we know nothing," he replies.

She nestles closer against him, yawning. "That's how we begin to learn. . . ."

5

The garage of the Czechoslovakian Consulate had been converted to a study-workroom, set apart and away from the main building which stands deep in the Hollywood Hills, in an old and gloomy section of town at the base of the Santa Monica Range. The main window faces an enormous display of letters set midway up the range and spelling the name of the film capital itself. For aesthetic and psychotic reasons, the display is riddled with bullets—a tribute, perhaps, to the collective psyche of the world of cinema. The first *O* of HOLLYWOOD, ferociously exhibitionistic, splayed and pockmarked by the effects of poisonous minds, seems to occupy an entire window.

And *O* is the alchemical sign of the infinite, thinks Dr. Jira, pushing a wisp of hair from her blue-gray eyes, then clasping her hands behind her back, enjoying the idle associations which the long flight from Prague have created.

Kunstermann, the driver, had brought her a letter in the diplomatic pouch, and Jira herself had decoded it in the automobile. She wasn't surprised by the contents; she'd realized their inevitability the moment she'd heard of the destruction of the Uzbek transmitter. She had marveled at such a destruction, marveled at the Israelis, though she kept her marvels

198

to herself. Thankfully, the Soviets had not invited her to the Uzbek transmitter. It was top security, they had said. Their refusal was also a way of keeping her in her place. Had the Soviets been less secretive, thinks Jira, I wouldn't be alive today. She toys with the letter on the table, smiling to herself:

WONDERNET BROKEN, the message began. SUGGEST STRICTEST CAUTION.

Obviously, she thinks with amusement. Would I sacrifice caution on the altar of Soviet ineptitude?

The Wondernet had been the code name of the chain through which the psychics were delivered to their destinations; in the West it had begun with Waldheim in Vienna, then Todi in Rome, Kazin in Israel. This year's chain. The paymaster had been Van Kessel, in Amsterdam. It had taken so much time to infiltrate the Refugee Agency, the most blameless, apolitical agency on the globe, to find the weak spots of its officers, then to wheedle, cajole, praise and, finally, extort. Pity.

From the moment the Uzbek transmitter had blown up in the Russians' faces, Jira was reasonably certain that the Israelis were on to their game and were using psychics as well. Van Kessel's death, so mysterious to everyone else but her, now appeared to possess all the signs. The transmitter blowup proved it. The Israelis must have discovered the bracelets and divined the crystals to be the most potent natural receivers and transmitters. The crystals would become the form of the future. The power trines she had created were programmed to become crystals, had become crystals. Life on the planet was going to depend upon the recognition of every facet of crystal. The copper base, into which her own crystals had been set, was a molecular ground, radiating the forcefield of the wearer, focusing it into the crystal.

To transmit and to receive.

The Israelis would have recognized this in a flash. Just as they most likely had recognized the missing member of Jira's own unit, Asher Berman.

After all, one man with a crystal is merely an idea. Two supply the force of the idea. The third gives it form. By substituting *their* man for Asher Berman, the Israelis had altered the direction of the force. They had jacked up their own broadcast beam, piggybacking the piggybackers; they'd sent the wave smashing right back in the Soviets' faces.

Marvelous, she thinks. And yet how could the Israeli psychic have created the third force without wearing a bracelet himself?

The answer is so simple, so absurdly simple. The psychic must have held onto the other bracelets, one in his right hand, and the other in his left—the male-female polarity—and acted as a ground. But in that case, the Soviet transmission should have buried itself.

Unless, thinks Jira, admiring the potency of the thought, unless the psychic collected the transmission into his own body, then forced it back out through the bracelets. It couldn't have happened any other way. What an idea. How had he thought of such a thing?

Dr. Jira finds the problem as fascinating as it is disconcerting. She would love to meet the fellow. They would have much to discuss. Not only about the wave but also about that freak cold spell. Such an option had not even been considered.

"Doctor?" Sârka cries, and the nervous manner in which she is toying with her glasses startles Jira. Sârka is a model of control, the only young woman Jira had ever trained with no gestures self-consciously cloying or seductive. "We've only a faint reading on Berman's bracelet."

Jira raises her eyebrows.

"Perhaps Mr. Berman is not wearing it now," she says distractedly.

Sârka glances worriedly at her companion, who shakes her head. "It's not that," Vasla begins. "There's *another* bracelet in the area. A second one."

Jira turns to the girl, surprised.

"It's true," Sârka concurs. "We have received no readings in Israel. But now there are *two* bracelets, here, in California."

"Are you sure of this?"

A foolish question—Vasla looks as if she were about to cry.

200

"No need to be upset," Jira adds calmly, in a singsong manner, and wondering: Am I walking into a trap?

"Doctor," the girl continues, "I don't wish you to think me nervous, but don't you believe we should do what we came to do, and at once? The readings are still far far apart, but sooner or later they won't be. . . ."

She senses me, Jira thinks. She senses me only too well. But Jira smiles, maternally. "Be patient, darlings. I promise you a good time." And she turns to the hill once again, staring at the large *O* on weather-beaten stilts. "I'd very much like to meet the wearer of that second bracelet, whoever it is. . . ."

"It's a *he*," the girls chime in, then glance at each other embarrassedly.

Jira nods coolly. "I'd like to meet *him*. I've the feeling he's the reason I've come to California. . . ."

"The signal is *very* strong," Vasla adds bleakly. "Please. Can we just do what . . . what we came to do?"

But Jira is elsewhere, thinking: What a prize this fellow could be.

6

Oliver Gad and Gwyneth Powys have taken a suite in the old wing of the Beverly Wilshire Hotel, in a section as out of time as it is limited in comfort. Still, thinks Gad, it's a damned sight better than that modern wing with its mental-institution colors.

Gwyneth had liked Southern California immediately, and for reasons Gad found excessively whimsical.

"It has no character whatsoever," Gad states harshly.

"And therefore an excellent place for magic," Gwyneth replies. "A place for the actively alchemical imagination."

"Bollocks," says Gad. He didn't want to hear the word "imagination" ever again. Gwyneth's use of it had stung him far more deeply than he would have suspected.

"But did you see those houses in Beverly Hills? Norman castles with Spanish patios? Japanese inns with Tudor roofs? It's fantastic!"

"The only view I enjoy is of the palm trees," he mutters, setting his clothes almost fastidiously on hangers. "And even they look out of place."

"I wonder what the people are like."

"If they're anything like their houses, I daresay they'd be unqualifiedly schizophrenic."

202

Gwyneth shakes her head. "But imaginative."

"Enough!" he barks, turning from the armoire. "If what's out that window is your idea of imagination, give me the simplicity of Coutts and Company, Park Lane Branch."

"My little banker," she laughs. "You're in the kingdom of cinema. Can't you enjoy the illusion?"

"That's another word I don't like," he mutters. "I'm on the firing line, and all you and Sefer talk of is imagination and illusion. Even when I project myself, the act is concrete. Practical."

Gwyneth doesn't bother to reply. She gestures toward the window. "Hungry?"

"Not really, Gwyn. What about you?"

"A bit. Why don't we go for a walk on that wide and exciting avenue? The one with all the European shops?"

Gad snorts, but concurs, scratching at the bracelet once again.

"Gwyn?" he asks, pausing by the door. "This bloody bracelet itches."

"Let me see. . . ."

Gad holds out his hand while Gwyneth turns over the bracelet, examining it carefully.

"Shouldn't itch," she says. "Ugly thing, isn't it? No aesthetic appeal whatsoever. Why would they have made it so ugly?"

"Of course," Gad snaps, "the bracelet's still active. Probably because we're near the other psychic now. . . ."

"But *he's* not active, is he?"

"Not consciously," Gad reflects. "I wonder. . . ."

"Wonder what?"

Gad shrugs. Has the Doctor indeed arrived? he muses.

"Close to home," he says, putting off any further thought. "That's probably what it is. . . . Still, it itches."

203

7

He's very attractive," Vasla whispers, and returns the master bracelet.

"So is the woman," Sârka replies.

"Did you see his eyes?"

"Sometimes Doctor looks that way," Vasla answers, putting the bracelet on the stand beside her bed.

"You're always thinking of Doctor."

"Doctor's been so nice. Still, that man *is* attractive. . . ."

"He has the power, too," Sârka adds thoughtfully.

"What do you think?"

"About his power?"

"Yes."

Sârka lies in bed, snuggled warmly against Vasla. She puts her arm about her, mechanically, for the warmth.

"If the woman has the power, too, they're only a pair. We're a trine."

"But Doctor hasn't used her own power for centuries."

Sârka smiles and brushes a wisp of Vasla's wheaty hair from her eyes.

"Centuries." She smiles. "You still believe in fairy tales. There are natural laws—"

"I believe it was Doctor made the Golem," Vasla interrupts urgently. "I even asked her once."

"And what did she reply?" Sârka disengages herself from the girl and props herself up on an elbow. How could Doctor even listen to this provincial?

"She said that to make a Golem, according to the legend, you must know the seventy-two names of God."

"I know the seventy-two names. We all do. Ancient Hebraic mantras."

"But you must know how to *pronounce* them. That's the secret. She said the secret lies in how you breathe the seventy-two names. One false breath, and nothing will happen."

"She didn't answer you, then."

"She only smiled."

Sârka stares thoughtfully at the ceiling. Then she sighs and turns to her friend. *"We* can make monsters and send them out. It's the same as the Golem."

Vasla shakes her head. "No, it's not."

"Why isn't it?"

"Our monsters don't possess the seventy-two names of God. Our monsters are pitiful, compared with the Golem."

Sârka thinks about the clay-man said to be lying even now in the attic of one of the Synagogues at Prague. According to the ancient story, the Golem had been given life only once: to counteract the pogrom the evil Cardinal had planned against the Jewish community. Telling the population that the Jews were using the blood of Christian children to make unleavened bread, the man actively had added yeast to the dough of anti-Semitism. The wise Rabbi, hearing the rumor, fashioned a Golem to defeat the hate-filled Gentiles. The Golem had destroyed nearly the entire city.

"If you think Doctor once fashioned the Golem, then you are saying that once upon a time Doctor was a Jew."

Vasla nods. It is so obvious.

"Isn't she?"

"Of course not."

"I know she is."

"If she were a Jew, why would she do what she is doing?"

"I'll tell you," says Vasla urgently. "To make the other Jews even stronger."

Sârka starts to giggle at her companion's innocence. Then her laughter drifts away. Is this not a possibility? After all, according to the Doctor, the alchemical law requires one to boil the prime matter until the precipitate appears, *the essence of the prime*. And there is something about the Jews' survival, the *boiling* of their history that did indeed produce a tougher, stronger people. Is the Doctor speeding their evolution even further?

"That's an odd thought," says Sârka puzzledly. Then she remembers a remark she'd overheard. Jira had said that by his deeds Hitler had delivered the favored of God to Israel. And who was Hitler's chosen philosopher, the most potent bigot of the Third Reich? Alfred Rosenberg, himself a Jew. A curious remark, and one she hadn't at the time understood.

"Sârka, listen!" Vasla is tugging at her arm. "Sârka, if you don't believe me, why don't *you* ask?"

"What?"

"Ask Doctor if she is a Jew."

But Sârka shakes her head.

"Not now. . . ." Wondering how she would react were she to discover such a hideous thing. If Dr. Jira turned out to be a Jew, Sârka would waste no time. She would kill her, using the most awful tricks she had learned, devices Doctor herself had taught her. She would make sure she died slowly, hideously, and that she'd be there to watch.

"When it's time, I'll ask," she whispers, turning away from her friend and sensing, in an awful intuition, that Doctor, good Doctor, sweet Doctor, had already betrayed her. She shivers slightly. Vasla curls up beside her and is soon asleep, mouth open, breathing heavily, deeply.

Sârka lies awake, staring at the moon illuminating that strange and ugly series of letters outlined in the evening's light against the hill.

"I'll do horrible things to her," she whispers, and feels her eyes beginning to water. "Even though I love her every bit as much as Vasla, I'll have her screaming."

The strength of her emotion, and of Vasla's, is in its own way understandable. For they are, both of them, merely fifteen.

8

The rehearsal studio is in the heart of Hollywood, on Santa Monica and La Brea boulevards, not five miles from where Jira is quartered and less than ten miles from Gad's hotel.

Asher is exhausted, but at the sight of Celia's musician friends in their farmer-outlaw-clown costumes, he becomes manic and filled with comic exhilaration. This is truly ridiculous; Asher's vision made flesh! What an impossible soup is America! And these fellows aren't even American; rather, a dadaist's abstraction of the place, a surrealist's drama in which these insanely dressed musicians appear as allegorical figures. Brecht, he thinks, couldn't have written them better.

Celia introduces everyone quickly and with so many endearing nicknames that Berman is sent spinning. Then, just as swiftly, she is at the piano, playing the melody of "California Glances." Once through, no lyrics. The five clowns leave their slouching, take up their instruments and begin to improvise around the theme.

Suddenly Celia slams her hands on the keyboard. "Shit, guys, learn the goddamn thing before you jam!"

She turns to the keyboard once again and this time sings the piece through slowly. The bass player starts to laugh, shaking his head.

"Jesus," he says. "The love song to end all love songs," and turns to Asher brightly. "Did *you* write that?"

Asher nods, slightly embarrassed.

"Outasight, man!"

"Is this a compliment or an insult?" asks Asher, blank-faced, and everybody laughs.

"What we gotta do," Celia begins, "is to play the thing straight, see? Like I'd even want some strings in here, you know, the way McCartney did 'Yesterday'?"

"Yeah, Ceel, but that was a bowed bass," says one of the musicians.

"A cello," another corrects.

"Well, we could start with the strings," Celia continues, "then drop 'em out when we get to the lyrics. Afterward I'd like to bring 'em in for a four-bars coda."

"Easy and out," says the musician called Ken, and makes a thumbs-up sign to Asher.

During the first minutes of their duet Asher is extremely nervous. His voice cracks. He softens it, covering his fatigue by whispering lyrics and musical line. Their voices, his and Celia's, begin to intertwine, to make love, to dance within a forest of soft and dappled shade. And when it is done, and they are staring at each other still, transfixed, Ken sighs, whispering, "New phase, Ceel."

And Asher knows he has been accepted.

He turns happily to Celia.

But she is shivering.

"Celia?"

But the singer is staring inwardly.

The Void, the womb of Celia's Great Mother, has been penetrated by another force, which, like a fisherman, is setting hooks into the base of her spine. Celia had drawn upon the fruits of the Void for sustenance; she had channeled the vibrations into song; the Great Mother provided so many melodies, and now she has gone. And in her place a swirl of forces helping an entity to set hooks into the base of her spine, to channel a song of a darker nature.

Asher watches Celia helplessly.

For an obscure reason, he wishes he were still wearing his bracelet. As masochistic as it is. As nostalgic.

"What have they done with Mother?" Celia Graves is whispering, her face bathed in harsh and oily sweat. "I don't see Mother anywhere. . . ."

9

Gwyneth is driving the car.

Gad holds Selliger's bracelet, eyes closed, reaching out for the faint feeling that seems to emanate from the north, at a spot beside the ocean.

"Keep it straight," he whispers, "along the coast."

"Beautiful here," says Gwyneth quietly. "Just look at it."

But Gad remains with his eyes closed.

"Shhh," he says. "Let me feel it. . . ."

The signal is so very faint that he knows something is wrong.

"Right," he says. "He's not wearing the damned thing. Small wonder."

Then he becomes aware of another signal and is startled.

"Stop the car," he says quickly. "Pull it over. . . ."

Gwyneth maneuvers the automobile below a cliff, oblivious to his tone, and stares happily about her. Trucks and autos whiz by her as if she were a fleck of dust on the road.

"Now why should I be getting two signals?" he wonders. "This one I know, this first one. I picked it up in Israel. I'm certain it's Berman's. But there's something—" He feels the hackles rise on his spine. Quickly he rips off the bracelet and tosses it out of the car, to land at the base of a concrete strut.

210

"Move!" he yells, and slams his left foot down atop Gwyneth's. The car lurches forward, onto the highway as a truck lets loose with a blast from its air horn and swerves onto the other lane.

"Gad!"

"Keep it going. . . ."

He turns around, noting a house hanging absurdly over a cliff, with half a swimming pool, tennis court and portion of the Hawaiian-style home leaning like a drunken sailor into space, supported by concrete pilings.

"Omigod," he whines as the concrete struts appear to change their nature, to become rubber, and the swimming pool catapults end over end over the cliff, burying itself in the loose earth beneath; as the tennis court follows, smashing into myriad bits of asphalt over the pool and onto the highway itself; as the building slides over the top of the mountain, holding for an instant and then plunging onto the rubble, living room accordioning into bedroom, bedroom into kitchen, then both hanging by water and gas mains almost comically and then snapping off and tumbling below the spewing jets of arching water. Then the cliff itself, relieved of its burden, yet lonesome for companionship, follows, embracing house and highway, and sending motorists over the edge and onto the beaches.

"Gad!"

But Oliver Gad is not listening; is shaking, giggling hysterically.

"What did you do, Gad?"

"Keep driving, darling. I'm afraid we have visitors. . . ."

In the distance, fire sirens begin to serenade the citizens of Pacific Palisades.

"Clever of you," she says, "to wear an exploding bracelet."

"Well?"

Sârka turns from the workbench to Dr. Jira. Vasla is still concentrating on the tiny bracelet, staring hard into the crystal.

"We lost them for a time," says Sârka.

Jira nods politely, waiting.

Vasla sighs, leaning back into her chair and stretching. She glances at Sârka with amusement.

"Then we caught them," she says.

"And?" asks the doctor. Most quietly. Most patiently.

Both girls begin to giggle.

"And we got them."

10

They are seated in a coffee shop in Trancas, along the beach, quietly sipping their tea.

"Now that we've lost the bracelet," Gad is saying, "we haven't a clue. We don't know where Berman is, where Jira is. Then again, they don't know where we are either. You know, Gwyn, I think we should do something no one seems to have done thus far."

Gwyneth looks up, amusedly. "Dematerialize the State of California and bring it back to London for inspection?"

"Not quite," Gad snorts.

"I should have brought Astrud and Lizaveta with me."

"Could, should, can," Gad mutters. "Why don't we simply use our heads?"

Gwyneth grins. "The brain is not the only organ of cognition, Gaddy."

"Well it's the only one I've got, ducks. Let's start from the beginning."

The waitress, whose skin is leathery from the sun, whose hair is wiry from peroxide, moves like a sand crab to their table.

"You folks are English, aren't you?"

"Perfect example of the brain at work," Gwyneth whispers.

213

"Yes," Gad replies politely. "And we'd like some more tea."

"I could tell you were English," the waitress replies. "Your clothes are different."

Gad nods and turns his back upon the woman.

Gwyneth is grinning at his frustration. "Very well," she says. "Why did Berman come to Los Angeles?"

"Right," Gad replies. "He's a singer. All things being equal, a singer comes to Los Angeles to make records."

"But for which recording company?" Gwyneth asks.

Gad tosses his shoulders angrily. "I don't know. But who came to Israel to see him? All things being equal, someone in the record industry. . . ." The whole thing is stupid, he feels. But it's an hypothesis. Work with it.

"From the beginning," he whispers to himself. "Asher comes to Israel. Someone meets him. He flies to California. Who is on the flight with him? Who sits next to him on the plane? Does he speak with anyone? It has to be someone important, I'd imagine. It can't have been a nonentity, or he couldn't have left the country. What celebrities were on the plane? Forget it. Forget the Israelis *and* the plane. Here's what we'll do: Call every recording company and ask if Berman has a contract. Enough of the old *Abra,* Gwyn. Let's use the voice of sweet reason. Let's be unimaginative, dull and plodding. Let's be concrete, shall we?"

"Once more round the island . . . ," she sings.

"Right!" he replies, and waves to the waitress for their bill. "Better still," he adds. "D'you have a phone directory?"

"Sure thing," says the waitress.

"One with the listings of businesses?"

"Over here we call it the Yellow Pages."

"Excellent."

As the waitress leaves, Gwyneth leans into Gad with mischief on her features. "Planning to dowse the record companies with your right hand, as you would a stock or gilt?"

"Right you are," snaps Gad.

"So much," Gwyneth adds, "for the brain."

214

11

The Czech Consul has placed the limousine at their disposal. Jira and her minions are driving along the Pacific Coast Highway, following the weak signal from Asher Berman's bracelet. Jira is seated in the rear between the pair, holding hands with the both of them, quietly generating a force field to equal their own, to boost their ability to pick up the signal. She is calmer now. Berman will have to be the prize: to discover where he went wrong. To fix the broken part so it will never happen again. Pity about the other psychic. It would have been nice to meet him. . . .

The limousine continues north beyond the Malibu pier, eventually passing the coffee shop in which Gad and Gwyneth are poring over the Yellow Pages.

"It's closer," chime the girls. But Jira, steeped in her own problem, merely nods.

"We have it!" they shout.

12

See here! This is Mr. Gad of the British Consulate. Let me speak with the president of your record company at once."

The voice on the end of the line is hesitant, nonplussed. "Mr. Weston isn't in."

"Are you absolutely sure?"

"Yes. He's in New York."

"May I have his number?"

"Certainly. . . ."

Immediately Gad projects himself across the telephone wire, moving behind the secretary, watching her run through the files. He spots Celia's name, and Asher's penciled in beside her own; he puts his mind on her name, and that is enough. He sees her.

"I happen to know Miss Graves is at a rehearsal studio," he snaps, cutting off the secretary. "She has a most serious charge about to be issued against her in the United Kingdom, and which we are willing to drop. But I must speak with her at once."

The secretary is stunned. "But don't you want Mr. Weston's number?"

"If you value your job, young woman, you'll tell me where that studio is—right now!"

"At Sunshine Recorders. The corner of La Brea and Santa Monica. What did you say your name was?"

But Gad has hung up, and is staring triumphantly toward Gwyneth:

"In the future," he snaps, "don't consult the stars. Consult the Yellow Pages."

"How did you know they were at a recording studio?" asks Gwyn.

But Oliver Gad, self-righteous and not in the mood for questions, is already out the door.

13

They sit in the limousine at the foot of the drive. Kunstermann, the chauffeur, turns to Jira, but the latter puts a finger to her lips. The chauffeur glances at the girls, whose eyes are closed in concentration.

The chauffeur clears his throat loudly, then straightens himself in the seat, looking dully at the chain-link fence before him, the heavy iron lock entwined at the double bars. What nonsense, he thinks.

"Empty," says Vasla. "The house is empty."

"Very well," Jira nods.

"But shall we do it?" asks Sârka. Jira nods once again. The chauffeur is stunned as the gate seems to snap open, the lock flying off and landing in a field.

"Drive please," orders Dr. Jira.

The chauffeur stares, openmouthed.

"I said, *drive.*"

Kunstermann presses on the gas, and the car moves slowly up the road, coming to a halt before the ranch house.

Sârka, Vasla and Jira begin to leave the auto.

"But if somebody comes?" whispers the driver worriedly.

"Nobody will come," Jira replies in her pleasantest tone.

As they cross up the walk, the chauffeur swears the door has opened by itself.

"I can't believe it," he mutters.

In spite of his years spent in Marxist analysis of history and human behavior, he crosses himself.

They stand in the foyer of the house, gazing vaguely about them. Then Vasla says, "Bedroom," and they move unerringly to that portion of the dwelling.

"Nightstand," Sârka calls.

"I saw it *first!*" Vasla claims.

Sure enough, there on the nightstand is the bracelet.

"*Now* what do we do?" asks Sârka, letting Vasla grab the copper bracelet as if it were a piece of candy.

"Give it back to Mr. Berman," Jira replies simply.

"Must we wait here?"

"Not at all. Put it back on that table."

Vasla sighs, complying with the order.

Then Jira takes Sârka's hand, and Vasla's, and the three of them stare hard at the bracelet.

In a minute it is gone. Dematerialized.

"Now make sure it *stays* on his wrist, darlings," orders Jira.

Sârka holds the master bracelet for a moment, eyes closed. Then she says, "Yes, it's strong. He has it now."

"Does he know?"

"Not yet."

"Send him love and good feelings. Wherever he is, keep him there."

"Shouldn't we destroy him now?" asks Sârka.

Jira, the artist, shakes her head. "We have already made a mistake. Never again. I need him to help us—if only to improve our technique."

Sârka frowns. But Jira gives her an encouraging pat on the shoulder.

They move to the living room and are surprised to find Kunstermann at the door, his hands raised in the air. Behind him stands a security guard with a pistol pointed at the chauffeur's back.

"Against the wall!" the man shouts. He is nervous. Terribly nervous. (Satisfyingly so, thinks Jira.)

Jira, Vasla and Sârka move to the fireplace. The guard shoves the chauffeur toward them and crosses to the telephone. (Such a young man, thinks Jira, to be so nervous.) Then she gives a slight nod to Vasla.

"What're you doing in this house?" stammers the guard, reaching for the phone. But the cradle jumps. He reaches again, and the cradle leaps even farther.

"What. . . ?"

Suddenly the gun turns red-hot, and he drops it, terrified.

Vasla is grinning. Jira nods to Sârka, who begins to stare at the young man. He cannot move. She keeps him there, fixed with her eyes, making encouraging motions with her head. Then Vasla crosses slowly to the guard and takes his hand, stroking it slowly. Though paralyzed, he feels the heat rush up his spine, oh, she is sweet, the way she is smiling.

Then he feels no more.

14

S hould we lay down a track?" asks Ken, but Celia shakes her head, fighting back nausea and the now uncontroll- able shivering, trying to keep from doubling in pain. "I'd like to sit on 'Glances,'" she struggles. "Until Weston comes back."

"But what about the duet? Come on, Ceel. . . ."

She turns to Asher worriedly.

"Whatever you wish," he says, misreading her look, thor- oughly at home now with the outlaws. He cannot recall ever being so happy in his life, save for those moments when he had been performing and the waves of laughter had swept over him like a warm and enveloping embrace.

"May we do the music now?" he asks.

But Celia is rubbing her head. She turns to the man in the booth. "Is Mike here?"

"No."

Suddenly Celia begins to scream, "Well, *get* him! Jee- zuss. . . !"

"What do we need Mike for?" asks Ken nervously. "We're only doing a single-track—"

"Because I *want* Mike, idiot!" she snaps, and her accent seems unmistakably British. The pain in her head has begun to recede.

Turning to the man in the booth, American-voiced again: "So get him, will you?"

The engineer nods with a kind of fatalism and leaves the booth.

"Ceel . . . ," Ken begins, but Celia is on the floor, on her hands and knees, heaving. It is as if a surgeon had pulled her spine up through a neat incision at the top of her skull and were replacing the spine with another, more refined version, one whose nervous system reached beyond the stars and into a dimension where order has reversed itself and harmony is an interloper. A cool and cleansing wind rushes through Celia's veins, lulling the pain, refreshing her pores. And then the operation is over. Celia gazes about with cold, glittering clarity. Asher rushes to her and is startled when she looks up calmly, eyes of an indigo he has never seen before.

"Nearly time," she growls. "Stay back, all of you. . . ."

Asher and the others watch her worriedly.

"Should I get a doctor?" whispers Ken.

Celia shudders, gives a tight, surprised sigh and rises suddenly, dusting herself. She stares at the others. "Not to worry," she says. "Well, then . . . are we going to record this song or aren't we?"

Ken nods, terrified. "Where did you get that voice?"

"Celia, please," says Asher. "I am in no hurry to—"

"Oh, Asher, don't be such a nit," she replies. "Since we've the power to enchant, enchant we must. Well?"

But the others only stare. Then, with a terrible triumphant glance from Celia Graves, they move like whipped pups toward their instruments.

"Much better," she says, hands folded at her chest. "Mustn't disappoint the guests."

15

C elia Graves?" asks Gwyneth, surprised. "The White Goddess?"

Gad nods, frowning, and turns off the Pacific Coast Highway and onto Sunset Boulevard. According to the map, Sunset should lead them into Hollywood. A quick dowse had also alerted him to the likelihood of light traffic.

"What's White Goddess?" he questions. "Another California salad dressing?"

"She's a singer. What's the matter with you, Gaddy, don't you listen to music?"

"Not much," he says. "Can't be too perfect, can we?"

"I heard her, once, in London. She's a channel, you know. And like most channels, she's absolutely emptyheaded."

"What is a channel?"

"It's a sort of medium. You're open to other entities, other planes. They work through you. Celia Graves sings about the Old Religion very well. A few of her songs led me to believe she had access to those planes."

"I wonder what Berman's doing with her? His name was penciled in beside hers."

"Didn't you say he is a singer?"

"That's Carmel's belief, yes. Obviously. He was going to do the broadcast."

Gad glances at his watch and wonders aloud: "A channel. Does she have the same powers as a witch?"

"Oh, God no," Gwyneth laughs. "A witch may also be a medium, but a medium is rarely a witch. In fact, mediumship can be quite dangerous. Witches live longer."

"Why?"

"Because sometimes mediums and spiritualists can be taken over by discarnate spirits. Which is why I've often counseled friends never to play with a Ouija board. You never know what may come through. And since a medium is generally in an unconscious state, the entity can often take over and remain in her body."

"Interesting," says Gad. "Then I'd watch my step, if I were you."

Involuntarily Gwyneth shudders and turns to Gad. He is frowning still, maneuvering the car out of a canyon and into a broad and treelined avenue.

"Why should I watch my step?"

Gad raises his eyebrows, cocks his head. He whispers something.

"What?"

"Leila Kent?" he enunciates as if he were a BBC announcer. Gwyneth pales and looks away.

"The signal is very strong," Vasla urges. "Tell him to turn left." Jira, yawning, snaps her fingers. The chauffeur, as near to madness as is possible, continues to follow orders. After what he has been witness to, the very act of driving an automobile is the only thing keeping him in touch with his senses.

"Yes, it's very strong," Vasla repeats.

Jira turns to Sârka, who is asleep, her head against her shoulder. Comfortingly, Jira puts her arm around the girl. Sârka always slept afterward. She required her rest. She'd be needing the power soon enough.

"A right turn, make a right turn," shouts Vasla, but the chauffeur overshoots the street.

"Pay attention," Jira hisses, and the driver nods, terrified.

Gwyneth says nothing. How had Gad known about Leila Kent? And what did he mean? From the moment Gad had mentioned her name, she had refused to look at him, feeling such overwhelming guilt. It wasn't fair. He could have waited before pulling the name from his infernal bag of tricks. She follows him out of the car and into the recording studio, head down, refusing to look at him.

Gad stops before the guard.

"Celia Graves, please," he drawls.

The guard looks up, his face an encyclopedia of boredom and defeat. "Who're you?" he growls.

"Mr. Weston's British counterpart," Gad snaps. "From 'swinging' London. Who are *you?*"

The man turns away—another defeat—and points. "Studio A. To your left."

" 'Kyou," Gad replies, and starts to move forward, then stops. "By the by," he says, "there are to be no more visitors to that studio. You're to say Miss Graves has gone for the day. Do you understand?"

The man nods glumly.

Gad turns to Gwyneth. "Coming?" he asks, holding out his hand.

But she refuses to take it.

They are in the middle of the duet when Celia Graves notices the young man with the silvery hair standing behind the controls engineer.

"Stop it at once," she says, and waves to Asher, cutting off the musicians. "This is a closed rehearsal," she calls. "Who let you in?"

The engineer turns around, surprised by the presence of

Gad and the attractive woman. Gad leans forward to speak, and the engineer points to a microphone.

"We're friends of Asher's," he says, flipping the control switch. Berman turns quizzically to Celia, shaking his head.

"Yes, well he doesn't know *you*. . . ."

Then Celia Graves spots the young woman standing beside Gad, and her eyes darken. Gad smiles politely, staring at the émigré.

"Asher? Dr. Jira—"

It is so pleasant, how it happens. Asher Berman has moved away from Celia and toward the glass, staring intently at Gad. Perhaps he is screaming. Gad can't remember. Not that it matters much, for there are two girls beside Gad, holding his hands and smiling up at him. Very pretty girls. One has round-rimmed glasses; the other hair the color of an autumn field, wheat-colored it is, and eyes set wide apart over high cheekbones. They are smiling with such familiarity that his groin begins happily to stir.

The man at the controls seems to be asleep. That is, his head is on the panel, eyes staring lazily at the glass. The others, the musicians, also appear to be asleep, perhaps they are dead, it is so very hard to tell, but it hardly matters. Asher is walking toward the door arm in arm with an extremely attractive woman, something familiar about her, the lushness of her features, the severe but pleasant cut of her hair, and Gwyneth, dear Gwyneth, appears to be waltzing with Celia Graves. Gad smiles dreamily at the waltz, the woman in white and the Welsh witch, it is so pleasant. How Gwyneth has left the booth he cannot remember; it doesn't matter, for these girls, this strange and gentle pair, are pulling lightly at his arms, are stroking his wrists. The one with the high cheekbones, he likes *her* well enough, good for the tumble, she is promising indeed—odd, but he feels as if he were about to have an orgasm.

The girls, both of them, have taken him to a dark place with a blue light, some part of a storeroom filled with tapes and reels, and are pressing against him lazily, always keeping his head up, and there is that soothing, embarrassing rush to his groin, and he seems to remember that criminals when hung also have erections, also have orgasms, and his neck hurts from the thought, and *damn!* he fights to break the contact with their eyes, but they keep spinning him about, oh, no, my darlings, he knows them now and pretends to buckle, feeling them both upon him, hands at his neck, wondrous hands holding him down, and so he falls, touching the length of them wheat hair to slim neck to tight little breasts struggling beyond the pink cotton sweaters, beyond the groin such possibilities steady and sweet to land at their ankles and that is all he needs now grabbing their ankles and tumbling them both surprise! and snatching the bracelet the girl with the glasses is holding, cutting the connection, rising quickly, releasing the grand old Ape to take care of the rest poor dears hearing them thrash as their little throats are crushed by the dutiful psychic simian, "Surprise," he whispers, for those sweet things have nearly killed him, but where is Gwyneth, Asher, what is going on? and so he staggers out of the closet, back down the corridor, past the stupid guard, noting the loll of his head, how the man's neck has been broken—little beasts!—and turning to the studio door, taking three deep breaths to clear his head, fighting the nausea, the stinking horror of his own near death, throwing open wide the metal door and screaming, "Gwyn-ethhh. . . !"

The woman in white and with her legs locked atop the Welsh girl has wrapped the guitar cord about Gwyneth's neck and is pulling it tightly, muscles straining, turning to the young man once and terrifying him with her wolverine snarl, her ancient, bony face whose skull pokes through her hair whose upper lip is missing whose eyes are blazing red whose tongue hangs like a dog's against her hairy cheek, so Gad intones from the depths of his soul, *"KENT-BE-DAMNED!"* and shoots his right arm out straight and feels the fire leap up in his back to surge through his muscles, carried by fierce and stinging nerves; like a bolt of lightning, it courses from his fingertips and dazes the woman, sending her slamming backward, spinning away from Gwyneth, flying in a tangle of bones to smash against the piano with a scream that raises the hackles of his back.

He dashes to his lover.

Scarred she is, and scratched as if by a jungle creature; he removes the cord from her neck, leaning against her chest, pushing hard, pushing long, crying, "Jesus, God, please help her"; he seems to be pushing her for hours until the color returns to her cheeks and he hears a faint whimpering sound; he continues to push until she is coughing, desperate for air, and her hands are making little circles at her side, and it is fine, she is alive, and he is crying, too, "Gwyneth, oh, God . . ." and her eyelids flutter as she reaches for his hand and slowly brings it to her lips.

"It's all right," he whispers. "It's fine," he is saying. "She's gone, Leila Kent is gone. . . ." He forces himself to turn toward the body at the piano.

Celia Graves seems to be sleeping peacefully, but for the blood trickling down from the corner of her mouth.

Dr. Jira sits in the limousine, waiting. Asher Berman, his eyes glazed and with a goofy smile upon his face, leans against the woman, enjoying her softness. Her hand, light and elegant, rests upon his knee.

"We *must* go," says the chauffeur. "Please."

"Not yet," Jira whispers, watching the studio door, hoping with pathetic innocence that her little friends will appear, arm in arm, laughing delightedly as they'd always done. But when the door does open and that strange man appears, the one with the silvery hair and clear blue eyes, she knows that she has lost her charges forever.

"To the airport," she urges, feeling the same animal fear that had overcome her only once in her life—when the death sentence had been read against her husband.

"But how can you take *him?*" whines the chauffeur, gesturing toward Asher.

"Get me a passport! Surely our people have one?"

The chauffeur nods, moving the limousine up La Brea and toward the Hills. Asher, like a lobotomy victim, watches the blur of traffic and continues to smile.

Could that fellow with the silvery hair possibly be the psychic? Jira wonders, and turns around to see.

But Oliver Gad has already disappeared.

16

The Israeli Consul turns from the telephone, cupping the receiver. A doctor is putting some kind of salve on the neck of the woman lying in the bed. The man with the silvery hair is seated beside her.

"The airport's been sealed," whispers the Consul. "Both at Burbank and at International."

"They're not at the airport yet," barks Gad, and the Consul frowns: "What are you? Psychic?"

Gad fingers the bracelet he had pulled off the wrist of one of the killer girls and closes his eyes.

"They're still in a car."

The Consul shakes his head. "Can you describe them?"

"Of course. . . ." Gad takes the phone from the Consul and gives Israeli Security a complete description of Dr. Jira and Asher Berman.

Wearily Gwyneth looks up at Gad from the bed. She tries to rise, but the doctor tells her to roll over.

"*Your* turn for vitamins," says Gad.

"Where are you going?" asks Gwyneth, wincing from the sting of the needle.

"Perhaps I'll borrow the Consul's driver," he yawns, "Follow the other fox. First, however, I'd like a bath."

Gad moves to the bathroom and locks the door; then he crosses to the tub and turns on the tap. Having removed his shoes, socks and pants, he sits at the edge of the tub, his feet in the warm water. In the event Dr. Jira senses his presence and sends a wave of destruction through the bracelet, Gad wants to be grounded in water to let the wave travel to his toes and to settle in the denser medium. It would be easier, Gad knows, to empty a bathtub of a psychic flash than to put out a hotel fire started by that selfsame flash. He fingers the bracelet in his hand and sighs, closing his eyes.

A round building, oddly colored; a range of mountains; and a sign reading HOLLYWOOD. Then Asher Berman, seated like a zombie beside that handsome woman, Dr. Jira. Asher is stirring, looking expectantly at Jira. Gad quickly releases the bracelet, not wanting to arouse Jira's suspicion.

After a moment he picks up the bracelet again.

The car is moving slowly through dense freeway traffic. *Good afternoon, Doctor,* thinks Gad, hanging onto the thought, beginning to whisper to the driver.

Jira, staring ahead, seems to notice nothing.

After fifteen minutes Gad returns from the bathroom and enters the suite.

"We thought you'd drowned," says the Consul.

"What were you doing?" Gwyneth asks.

"Shhh," Gad says, to the knock at the door of the suite. *"Mesdames et messieurs,* we are about to have a visit."

He crosses with a lively gait to the other room, where he swiftly opens the door.

"Enter," he says. "Please do, Mr. Berman. . . ."

Asher Berman, looking quite shaken, staggers into the room. Gad glances behind him, then yanks the white-faced chauffeur by the arm, to send him crashing into the doorjamb. But Gad is stunned. "Where's Jira?" he barks. The chauffeur, panting feverishly, tense and rigid, cannot speak. Quickly Gad clutches Asher's wrist. The bracelet is gone.

231

Gad rushes to the bathroom once again. His aplomb vanishes as swiftly as a summer storm. He wants Jira. He needs her desperately. There are so many questions, and only Jira has the answers. None of them, neither Gwyneth nor Julian nor Sefer could ever have the knowledge of that doctor from Prague.

Furiously Gad clutches the bracelet without even bothering to ground himself in water lest Jira send him a wave.

With Berman and Kunstermann moving like zombies into the hotel, Dr. Jira finds herself standing alone, confused, and holding an active bracelet. She moves to the side entrance, knowing that she must destroy the bracelet before it links her too uncomfortably with that lean and silver-haired man, that powerful and curious being. She attempts to send a vicious, stinging wave through the crystal but senses that it is slipping into a neutral medium. Useless, she thinks.

The fellow must be exceedingly practical. To think of grounding himself at such a time as this. To have destroyed Vasla and Sârka so quickly. Someone must have trained him. How quickly he learned. But if he was trained, if he learned, then his right side, his solar side, what the cabbalists call the Pillar of Mercy, the right channel must be overactivated. And his left? The lunar side, the channel of intuition? The Pillar of Severity? Surely he would not have had enough time to develop such a distinctly feminine channel?

Very well, thinks Jira. Let us assume his left side is as weak as his right is strong. He can attack or defend only from the right. The sun, too, must dream and live in its lunar reflection. Here's a dream, then, my dear. . . .

Dr. Jira turns toward the bushes lining the hotel, oblivious of the passersby. She begins to stare deeply into the crystal, feeling a cool thrust of silver from the base of her spine to the crown of her head. Bathing her being in silver.

After three minutes Dr. Jira sighs almost erotically, then tosses the bracelet with nonchalance into a gutter along the boulevard.

"There you are," Gad hears distinctly. The voice is calm, soothing, thoroughly reassuring.

"I wanted to meet you," Gad whispers, seeing the face clearly now, the wonderful lines, the cool blue-gray eyes, the sadness of those eyes and the rich, full mouth.

"Come to Prague," says the woman. "You're sure to find me there. . . ."

Gad tries to project himself but feels as if an invisible curtain of iron were hanging between them. "I'll meet you anywhere you wish," says Gad, "and as your equal."

The woman smiles, and Gad, or rather his double, finds himself on a boat heading out to sea. Where, he does not know, he cannot say. But the woman is seated at the stern, watching him with a certain pleasure.

"Why do you do it?" Gad's double whispers. "How can you do it?"

"Come to Prague. You're sure to find me there. . . ."

Gad shudders. The woman is starting to fade. Gad reaches out an arm to touch her, to connect. He needs her desperately, but his arm is stirring helplessly in the mist.

"Wait," he urges. "Please! From whom does the power originate? How have you countered metaphysics with physics, the Old Religion with science? How is it, with all you do, with all you're capable of doing, you've never evolved? We *do* evolve, don't we?"

"Come to Prague," the woman whispers. "You're sure to find me there." And she turns and gestures to the sky. Gad turns as well, to see a woman in white standing beside an altar, hands held out beckoningly.

"What?" Gad whispers.

"I'll meet you anywhere you wish," his double repeats. "And as your equal."

Jira vanishes. And with her, the woman of the moon.

Oliver Gad blinks, sees only himself in the bathroom mirror, his muscles white from clutching the bracelet, his stomach contracted to a painful knot, eyes filled with tears. He throws the bracelet angrily into the sink. Dumb. Lost. Stupid as ever, Gad. Foolish bastard. *You-know-nothing!*

The chauffeur is sobbing, his face buried in his hands. Asher is sipping some tea, looking confusedly about him. His eyes are clear, though he is very frightened.

"He's broken," says the Consul, pointing at the chauffeur. "Absolutely mad. Said something about being told by a ghost to drive to this hotel. That he'd opened the door to let out Berman and the doctor. That the doctor took something from Berman. . . ."

"The bracelet," the chauffeur sobs. "She took the bracelet. Then she went away. . . ."

Gwyneth sits up in bed, alarmed.

"Gad. . . ."

But Gad shakes his head. "Rubbish. The bracelet's lying in a gutter, down below, on that boulevard."

The Consul stares at Gad, surprised, but Gad's eyes remain locked into Gwyneth's. "I thought I had her. But she put out the same damned thought form as Sefer'd done. The same bloody trick. Left it in the gutter. Not a trace."

"Well," says the Consul, rising, "that means she's still in California. We're sure to find her."

"No," says Gad almost joyfully. "You never will. Not here." Then he turns to Asher, eyeing him with concern. "How do you feel?"

Asher looks up and shakes his head.

"Celia . . . ?" he whispers, turning away from the Englishman to the woman lying in bed. And yet he knows. From her features he *knows.*

"It is so stupid," he whispers, and tries to smile. "I had thought, for one instant of my life I had genuinely *believed* that happiness was not an invention of the middle class. I must be crazy. I am crazy, but I must have been crazier still. In the sense, of course, that the middle class is an invention of the lower class, which is by necessity an invention of the upper class, without which. . . ." His voice breaks. "But is she dead?"

"Yes," says Gad softly.

Asher nods, as if the knowledge no longer concerned him.

234

"Jolly good," he says, unconsciously mocking Gad's accent. "One less musician will never be missed. . . ."

They sit with him, long after the sun has descended, and a street-sweeping machine catches up the refuse on Wilshire Boulevard, crushing a copper bracelet with the ease of a god cuckolding mortality.

EPILOGUE

The deprogramming of Asher takes very long, and it bores Oliver Gad.

Rarely does he call Sefer. As long as the man is busy with Berman, going through the program devised by that exceptional Czechoslovakian Dr. Jira, Sefer has no need of Gad. Even Gwyneth is working continuously with Asher ("So *simpático*," she coos), taking Berman out-of-body to pick up clues for Sefer, to backtrack the deadly programming; she herself has little time for the Silver Fox.

Gad tries to renew his interest in Lombardy Street and the Exchange, but it is piss-poor, and he knows it. Sir Bill Boulter, after an angry dressing down for his absence, offers him the chairmanship of Lion-Elemental, the Anglo-Dutch chemicals merger ("Yes, by God, it was a *fine* thing, a brilliant idea of yours, ingeniously timed, as always")—but Gad refuses it as well.

So many things puzzle him.

Is he genuinely lacking in imagination, as they all say, or is he beginning to move beyond imagination? And the woman at the altar. . . . Who is she, now that she is starting to drift, night after night, on his mind screen?

I can do things by myself, in threes, he thinks. But why?

He feels dull.

He feels useless.

To Oliver Gad, life has become a puzzle and a bore.

To one more aware of intense psychic change, it is apparent that Oliver is beginning to spin toward the dark night of the soul, tripping through indescribable regions of time and space, before illumination.

And then one day Oliver Gad simply disappears.

Gwyneth is the first to be alarmed. Twenty hours later Sefer is worried as well.

"Do you believe that Gad—" but Sefer cuts her off and with such ferocity that Gwyneth is shocked.

"We're after knowledge," he spits. "Not *belief*. I don't give a damn about *belief*. Until we have knowledge, we have *nothing*. Is that understood?"

Gwyneth nods, "Yes. Quite. But still. If you have a *feeling*, you don't deny it, do you?"

Sefer does not bother to reply.

There is nothing to say.

It is May 12, a special day in the history of Czechoslovakia, a day of Liberation and Independence. A day of nostalgia. At the Prague Concert Hall the audience is listening to a work that gives them atavistic shudders: Smetana's *Má Vlast, My Fatherland*. It is so well known, so much a part of the land and of the great river of sorrow that is their heritage that they become as one. An enormous single-breathing organism. A group soul.

A pair of young titian-haired and freckle-faced twins, whose rapturous looks are indistinguishable from the rest of the audience, sit on either side of an attractive woman, each holding the woman's hand. Her eyes, too, are closed in private attention.

"And now comes *Sârka,*"she whispers, alluding to the wondrous Czech princess whose wrath was ferocious indeed. Spurned by her princely lover, Sârka and her maidens had enchanted the prince and his soldiers, lulling them to sleep with drink, then slaying them with such violence they'd become frozen in the glacier of myth.

As the orchestra plunges into the wildly dramatic theme foreshadowing Sârka's amorous rage, the woman opens her eyes with an expression of genuine amazement. The twins look up at once.

"Yes?"

"Yes," the doctor nods. "He has come. Do you feel him as well?"

"Yes," begins the first charge. "We feel him even now. . . ."

"Good," replies the doctor. "I was right. And so . . . he has come." With a smile of pure contentment, she settles deeply into the seat, releasing herself to the music. The young girl nudges her twin, grinning pleasurably, conveying her own excitement. The other girl tries desperately not to smile. Then both begin to giggle.

With a special quality of anticipation that is youthfully endearing, yet dangerously naïve.

End of the First Spiral of Gad